WELL FARED,
MY LOVELY

WELL FARED, MY LOVELY

LES DAWSON

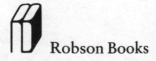

Robson Books

First published in Great Britain in 1991 by
Robson Books Ltd, Bolsover House, 5–6
Clipstone Street, London W1P 7EB

**British Library Cataloguing in Publication
Data**

Dawson, Les
  Well fared, my lovely.
  I. Title
  823.914 [F]

ISBN 0 86051 761 6

Typeset by Bookworm Typesetting, Man-
chester.
Printed in Great Britain by Butler &
Tanner Ltd, Frome and London

Once again, to my wife Tracy Poo for all the support, endless cups of coffee and love whilst writing this book. Also to Samson and Delilah, Thumper and Patch and Merlin and Muffin for just being around.

Acknowledgements

This stirring novel could not have been written without the help of these fine old institutions:

The Thyroid Clinic And Clay Elf Centre, Hull.
Moslem Pedal Bin Manufacturers, Gateshead West.
H. Cobbler & Son, Paper Hat and Clockwork Gherkins Ltd.

I would also like to thank Mrs Nokker-Jock for the use of her late husband's steam hammer and fruit welding apron; Miss Agnes Pyn for services rendered during a rehearsal for the Blitz; and all the boys at Chipping's bugle warehouse.

In particular, I would like to express my gratitude to Constable Wretch and his Auntie Jean for the use of their lavatory, and not forgetting the Joseph Von Pitchbaum Anvil Orchestra and Iraq Glee Club.

Last but never least, to Robson Books for having the guts to publish this novel. . . .

Les Dawson

Chapter One

'I always shampoo my gun because it's a hair pistol.

Nobody soft-soaps me – I'm too Bold for them, if you get my Dreft.

You can't sucker me, I'm not your Lifebuoy ... and Daz the truth.

I do this job just to Tide me over, it's hard work and after a case I just Flake out.

I'm no fool, although some people think I'm a silly sud.

Persilly speaking, it's a question of Ariel today and Calgon tomorrow.

I've just been handed a case and I'm Omo sure I can solve it.'

Marlowe

That Saturday night when it all began, I was sitting in my office ... the curtains were drawn but the rest of the furniture was real. I remember that I'd mixed myself a

9

cocktail which I called a Little David. Very strong – if you drink more than two you have to Goliath down.

Suddenly my ears started to ring. When I answered them, the call was from a private eye who had a pupil named Iris. He told me that a Russian spy had broken into an atomic laboratory and he'd stolen isotopes, dozy dotes and little lambs eat ivy. It was serious all right. I'd once worked in an atomic power station ... on Wednesday I'd made heavy water and on Friday I'd made light water ... trouble was, I couldn't find the uranium and I pee'd up a chimney.

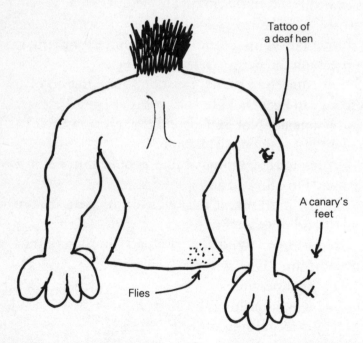

Rear view of Mussels Malloy. Sketch taken from a photograph of him at a Birmingham holiday camp during a tram exhibition.

Just at that moment, a letter was pushed under my door. It brought tears to my eyes – it was written on an onion. Before I could read it, there was a tap on the door ... I knew then that I'd have to have a word with that plumber. The door opened slowly, and there stood one of the biggest men I've ever seen. His nose was so flat his moustache was under his ears, and he had a very interesting left eye – the right one kept looking at it. His shirt was open at the neck and I've never seen such a hairy chest. He looked like a burst sofa. What really worried me was the way he was cracking walnuts with his eyelids.

'Are you Marlowe, the private dick?' he asked in a voice that sounded like a canary having a bowel movement in a tin. (I hate that word 'dick'. Being a private detective isn't an easy job ... not every Tom or Harry can be a Dick. In my time, I've been shot, stabbed and poisoned. Not any more – the wife went back to her mother.)

I muttered something and he shook me warmly by the throat. He allowed me the courtesy of breathing then poked me in the chest with a finger that was the size of a pork Scud missile. 'I'm Mussels Malloy, and I want you to find Velma.' With that, he sat down on my lap and sang 'Moon River' whilst showing me a card trick.

The big ape worried me. For a start he couldn't sing, and he was squashing the ferret in my truss. Somehow I managed to get him off my knee with the promise of a toffee, then I pulled my gun out and snarled 'Stick 'em up.' He said, 'Stick what up?' and for the life of me, I couldn't remember the next line. By then it was too late;

he took my gun and ate it ... he'd have bad wind later, my gun is a repeater.

Mussels gave me fifty pounds in ten-pence pieces and tap danced out of the office on the back of a pony that I keep for kicks.

Who the hell was Velma? I had to find her, otherwise Mussels would return with a three-piece band and croon a Des O'Connor ballad.

I was about to leave the office (I knew I was leaving because the office was going further away from me) when suddenly – and it might have been even quicker than that – a heavily veiled woman walked in smoking a roll of bacon and carrying a sack of wheat on her back.

'Hi, handsome.' Her voice was vibrant and low. Not surprising: she was a dwarf.

'What's the sack of wheat for?' I asked her.

She spat a length of bacon rind out and whispered, 'I'm looking for an all-night windmill.'

I couldn't help her. The windmill I used had closed down and was now a permissive launderette.

Before I could answer, she went on, 'I've been in the USA.'

I said, 'United States of America?'

She shook her head. 'No, flatfoot, upstairs in't attic.'

She came towards me, jumped up on the desk and started to lick my cheek. I said, 'Why did you do that? Do you fancy me?'

She answered hoarsely, 'No, I need the salt. Keep away from Mussels,' she went on, menacingly.

I didn't have to be told that, I hate sea food and once threw up after eating an oyster pie. My mysterious visitor walked crab-wise to the door then threw fifty pounds in ten-pence pieces into my black French beret. It hurt because I still had the beret on.

When she'd gone, I sat down with my pipe and smoking jacket, but I couldn't get the sleeves in the bowl so I lit up a cigarette instead.

Garish street signs threw bold fingers of illumination across my office window and caused shadows to flicker in the darkness of my small domain. I felt a cold chill run down my spine, then I realized that I'd taken off my beret and put on a ten-gallon stetson and it had sprung a leak. I swam out of the brim and curled myself up in the spin dryer and revolved for ten minutes.

I rummaged through my desk and found a pistol that I hadn't used in years because I'd run out of powder and shot. With it being two feet long, I had difficulty shoving it in a holster, so I glued it down my leg and walked out on a crutch.

I'd only walked seventeen miles when I realized I was being followed by a bald nun on horseback, and behind her, three market gardeners with shovels and buckets. I hid in a doorway until the nun had galloped by, then hailed a cab. 'Taxi!' I shouted, and the driver shouted back, 'Yes, it is!' and drove off.

Why was I being followed? Could it have anything to do with Mussels and the missing Velma? I had one clue. Mussels Malloy, I noticed, had a tattoo on his arm. I'd seen it when he was hitting the high notes of 'Moon River'. As he was taking a bow, I'd taken a photograph of it. I made my way to a chemist to have it developed. It was all I had to go on, so I stood on the roll of film and propelled myself down the street with the crutch.

I'd known Jake the chemist for years. When his wife had run off to sea with a draughtsman, I'd found him drinking glass after glass of carrot juice … dangerous stuff, you can get drunk on it very quickly, but at least you can see better.

Jake was happy to see me and it was obvious that he was getting on with his life. His wife was eaten in the Amazon but the draughtsman had returned home and he and Jake were now engaged. It's not for me to moralize, but they didn't seem suited. The draughtsman played a piano accordion in bed and it kept chipping the paint off Jake's trombone.

I'd taken a good snap. The tattoo was clear to see and the draughtsman fell in love with the arm.

The words 'The Ace Club' formed the main motif of the tattoo and I reasoned that was where I had to go. I bade Jake a tearful goodbye and the draughtsman played me out on the piano accordion with a sea shanty. Actually, he was quite good; I took my shoes off and performed the hornpipe. A small crowd gathered and Jake took a hat round and collected fifty pounds in ten-pence pieces.

I found The Ace Club in a back alley. What a dump. I knocked on the heavily barred door. It was opened by a man dressed as a sheep. He said, 'You can't come in – you're baaahed.' I gripped him by the wool and forced my way in. The room was full of smoke and the customers were all dressed as animals. I sat down and a cow served me a large pink gin. I looked around me and what I saw, I didn't like. Five roosters were dancing to a one-armed violinist, and a goat in suspenders was kissing a boa constrictor.

I ambled over to the bar, carefully avoiding a heap of plastic manure, then slipped on the real stuff. The man behind the bar in a bull's head gazed at me in surprise as I placed five pounds in ten-pence pieces in his hoof.

'Does the name Velma mean anything to you?' I said.

The bull snorted and shook his horns, but I sensed that he had been thrown by my question. Out of the corner of my eye, I saw a chimpanzee and a wild pig sidle towards the bar where I sat. Before I could speak, they'd hustled me behind the bar and through a door that led into what appeared to be a stock-room. A single fly-splattered bulb was the only source of light.

'Listen, flatfoot,' said the chimpanzee, 'why are you asking about Velma?'

I managed to break away from the half-nelson the wild pig had on me. I tore off the chimpanzee's head ... and lo and behold, it was the bald nun.

The wild pig struggled out of his costume and I saw a man emerge, a broad-shouldered man with ears so big he looked like a wingnut. I pulled out my pistol and a length of skin from my thigh, screamed a little, and asked them if they knew the telephone number of BUPA. I remember the nun hitting me across the head with a set of iron rosary beads, and I swam deep into a pool of unconsciousness.

When I surfaced in an ocean of pain, I was alone and tied up in a chair. I managed to start picking the back of my left hand with my right thumb, and soon I'd created a sore. With the sore, I cut through the ropes and freed myself.

The door was locked. That didn't bother me. My years spent in a Shaolin monastery near Kidderminster learning kung fu, karate and double glazing hadn't been in vain. I shoved ten pounds in ten-pence pieces under the door, and when the guard outside opened it I smashed my crutch in half with the side of my hand. Now I had two pieces of wood to hit him with. The brute went crashing to the floor – he'd tripped over the ferret which had slid out from my truss.

I panted my way out of that room, leaving the ferret to crawl up the unconscious guard's trouser leg. I don't know how far up it went, but I heard the man whisper, 'How much for the night?'

I made my way out of the club and walked back to the office, but I wish now that I'd walked forward instead. The hairs on my neck curled as I approached the office. Like a fool, I'd left the hot curlers in. I poured myself a drink, another concoction of mine which I call the Card Table Cocktail – if you drink more than three, your legs fold under you.

A shadow darted into my vision ... it was Mussels, and he was good and angry.

'Have you found Velma yet?' he hissed as he commenced to throttle me. He dropped me back into my seat, sat in the chair opposite the desk and put his head in his massive hands. He remained silent as I choked back to life. 'Sorry, Marlowe ... but jeeze, I love that dame.' He started talking as if to unburden himself of some secret grief. He was so boring, I left him for an hour and booked in at a hotel for a kip. When I got back he was still sitting there talking and I could hear a mouse snoring. This is his story. . . .

He was born into utter poverty. His mother was a music-hall artiste, part of an act called 'The Martha Haggett Trombone Romany Dwarfs.' She used to yodel Beethoven's Fifth Symphony whilst juggling with loose soot, and she was so short-sighted she wore braille socks. His father was very superstitious and wouldn't work if there was a Friday in the week. He came from a broken home: everything they used they broke. The only thing left in good condition was the bath. Mussels was one of ten children and the only way his mother could feed them all was by throwing a pan of soup into a fan.

Despite the conditions, Mussels grew into a giant. All the clothes he wore were cast-offs and hand-me-downs; at fourteen he went around in a bib, romper suit and pith helmet. He was lucky – when his sister got married, she stood at the altar in spats, football shorts and a bowler hat.

At fifteen, Mussels turned to crime and tried to do a smash-and-grab raid at a jeweller's shop. He was arrested for stealing a brick to smash the window with.

After being released from reform school he became a cat burglar, but his mother got fed up with so many cats in the house and Mussels had to leave the nest, as it were. In turn, he became a member of a street gang, a prize fighter and a wrestler, and his huge strength petrified all who met him. Girls avoided him like the plague and the only time he got his leg over was when he mounted his bike. He became a bodyguard for gangsters and a bouncer outside a Darby and Joan Club.

He was caught stealing a roll of elastic bandage and did a stretch in prison. He asked his mother to bake a cake and put a file in it. His mother said, 'The file's no problem, son, but how do you bake a cake?'

They liked him in prison; so much so that when he finally went straight, they asked him to go back in part time. Then one night (he didn't say where, or if he did, I didn't hear him) he met Velma.... She was everything he'd ever dreamt of ... thick black hair down her back (although there wasn't much on her head) ... a breath-taking figure: forty-nine, thirty-eight, forty-nine – and that was just her neck. Oh, how he loved Velma ... the fun he had had with her, the way she could stand in a hot pan of chips and imitate a dip-stick.

What Mussels didn't know was that she was sleeping around with other men and laughing behind his back. Nobody dared to tell him that. He held up banks to provide her with clothes and diamonds, but she kept on demanding more from him. The banks got so fed up with him, they started posting money off direct to Velma. Eventually she opened her own bank, and did all right until Mussels robbed it. That did it. She framed him for riding his bike through a park without lights. He went back to jail, and never passed go.

As Mussels brooded in prison, Velma vanished from the scene. Word on the street had it that she'd opened a bordello in Huddersfield, catering for geriatric greengrocers hooked on celery. Some wiseacres said that she'd gone bald in a cupboard during a riot outside Mothercare.... Nobody knew where she was, and Mussels brooded on in solitary confinement.

As soon as he was paroled, he took up the search for his beloved Velma, and that's when I came into the picture. By the time Mussels had finished telling me this sad story, a week had flown by and I now suffered from insomnia, foot cramp and stiffening of the eyelids.

I just had to get rid of him. At all costs, I had to find his bloody Velma.

A chance remark from a retired clown in the Polish Embassy led me to a riverside gambling casino in Oldham. The joint was owned by a man with a withered arm, one eye, one leg and piles who answered to the name of 'Lucky'. I posed as a wealthy man-about-town who liked a flutter, and to prove it I did an impression of a butterfly.

Casually, I mentioned the name Velma, and immediately, the one-legged man hopped away, only to return with two big men carrying baseball bats. People screamed as they hit me with the bats, forcing me to duck beneath the craps table. The smell under there was indicative of the name.

Somebody must have called the police because I heard a constable shout, 'What have you been calling me?'

I was pulled from beneath the table by a plainclothes 'tec called Mike Mallet. He didn't like me very much, not since I'd solved the case of the unknown applause in the burial chamber. That case became known as 'Who Crept in the Crypt, Clapped and Crept out Again?'

'Okay.... Whatta isa going on 'ere, hey?' he said in broad Italian.

I said, 'What are you talking like that for, Mike? You come from Preston.' Before he could reply, I saw the one-legged, one-eyed man with the withered arm and a botty full of Farmer Giles lying dead on the floor.

Mallet pulled me close to him by dint of grabbing my lapels. 'Listen, Marlowe, I want some answers – *now*.' He threw me into a chair as he spoke. I knew he would not be fobbed off; besides, he was still holding my lapels. They had parted company from the main body of the suit. I half rose to ask for my lapels back but Mallet pushed me down into the chair. As he withdrew his mitt, his watchstrap snagged on my shirt cuff. My sleeve slithered down from inside my jacket and hung from Mallet's wrist.

A rage boiled within me. I jumped out of my seat and swung at Mallet's chin. He swayed back, and as I fell on my knees I heard my braces snap. As I was jerked to my feet, my trousers dropped around my ankles and somebody pulled my fedora over my eyes, then had the nerve to hand me the hat brim.

'I'm watching you, gumshoe,' spat Mallet. He strode off as the medics removed the body of the one-legged, one-eyed, withered-armed man in a bin liner.

A white-faced cigarette girl lent me her frock, and as it clashed with my torn jacket she sold me an angora cardigan. It toned nicely with the floral pattern of the

C & A frock, although frankly it was too long for my taste.

It was raining outside the casino and I tried to flag a cab. Most of them had flags already covering them. Suddenly, I was pulled into a shop doorway and pressed against the glass window. I struggled to get free, but it was useless: my attacker had the strength of a grizzly bear. By the light of a passing bus, I saw that my attacker was none other than Mussels Malloy.

'Gee, you're beautiful,' he breathed in my ear as he started to fumble with the hem of my frock.

'Mussels!' I yelled. 'Stop it! It's me – Marlowe.'

He started singing 'Moon River', and as he tried to remove my angora cardigan he kept whispering 'Velma ... Velma.' I had to do something fast, his singing was crap. 'Have you got any tinted condoms?' I said sweetly.

He shook his head and lumbered off to a chemist's shop, first indicating that I should stay put in the doorway. I looked around wildly and saw a tramp lurching past. Almost without thinking, I dragged him into the doorway and knocked him out with a paving stone that just happened to be there (just as well really, otherwise there would have been no story). I stripped his rags off and dressed him in the frock and cardigan, then I crept around the corner as Mussels came back with a family pack of rubbers. I hightailed it away and followed a Salvation Army band to a soup kitchen, where I enjoyed a bowl of lentil soup and a slice of Hovis.

I didn't sleep well that night. I kept dreaming that I

had turned into a set of Meccano and Mussels was chasing me with a spanner shouting, 'Come back while I tighten your nuts.'

I got out of bed and it dawned on me that perhaps I was going deaf because I had stood on the cat. Wearily I put the kettle on then took it off. I looked ridiculous with it on, and my arm was stuck in the spout.

The newspapers were full of the murder at the Oldham casino and I cursed when I saw a photograph of myself on the front page: it was one taken when I was in the Scouts. On the back page, in the list of weddings and engagements, I read to my horror that Mussels Malloy had got engaged.

It had turned noon when I arrived at my office, and as I walked through the door, I tensed. There was a pile of horse shit on the carpet. There was no sign of the bald nun.

Something still wasn't right. Although I was alone in the office, I felt a presence. I was taking no chances. I'd put my two-foot pistol in for part exchange for a cannon and I commenced to pour powder on to the pan. The man who'd sold it to me only had three cannon-balls left, so I'd have to be sure of what I was firing at.

I went into the other room where I kept my files and all sorts of personal bits and pieces.... Photographs of my family, letters, my old Army uniform – the one I wore at my court martial when I was accused of staying in bed late. I remember hearing the commanding officer say to me, 'I say, Marlowe, don't you hear the bugle playing reveille in the morning?'

I'd shaken my head and replied nervously 'No, sir, I'm

always asleep when it's played.' They'd obviously gone into my family background because they discharged me from the Army a week later. . . .

I'd better explain.

I come from a strange family tree. One of my ancestors was Eric the Peculiar, the first Viking to get mugged in Gateshead. He married Winifred, who made chamber pots for the Iceni tribe, and was widely known as Winnie the Po. They begat Lame Leonard, who apparently was so ugly as a baby that his father put shutters on his pram. Winnie was so ashamed of the way her son looked, she used to put him upside down, naked, in his trolley and everybody thought the little lad had a cleft chin and bags under his nose. His parents couldn't afford talcum powder for his bottom so they used to roll him in self-raising flour. He never had nappy rash . . . he used to break out in jaffa cakes.

At quite an early age he became an idiot and did very well at it. At the age of forty-one, his mother left him on a doorstep and ran away. As it turned out, things improved for Leonard, and when he was forty-six he lived in sin with a lady idiot and they had six children but ate two of them.

Three of his kids were girls; they were sold to a Roman circus where they indulged in sex with elephants. Nero thought they were a great act and said that if there were any children as a result, they could be brought up as Methodists.

The fourth child, a boy, was like his father in looks.

At school he used to get little girls in the playground and say to them, 'Give me a kiss or a penny.' By the time he was fourteen, he owned his own house and a super-market.

His name was Alf the Cretin, and he made a living frightening truants on a Ghost Train. Oddly enough, despite having to wear a bag over his head in public, he met and married Doris, the daughter of a horse strangler in Potter's Bar. They had a boy child who was as handsome as could be. They christened him Rover because they had always wanted a dog, and he was house-trained at an early age. The trouble was, he was trained to do his motions in the house and the smell was so atrocious, they were rehoused in a brick kiln. Rover lost his mum and dad – they hadn't died, he'd just lost them – and grief stricken, he sailed to China one day. It was a terrible journey; he was strapped to the tiller with a sex-starved gorilla, and China's a bloody long way.

Right up to the present time, cowardice has been the cornerstone of the Marlowe character. My great-great-grandfather fought with Wellington – they couldn't trust him with a gun. During the Battle of Waterloo, whilst waving a white flag before the battle started, he had so many cannonballs peppered into his buttocks, they didn't bury him, they weighed him in for scrap. In the First World War, my Uncle Harry was on the Somme when the first shot was fired. He was under a couch in Crewe when the second one went off. Rumour has it that he had so many white feathers sent him, he played the Grand Theatre Leeds for two years as Mother Goose.

During the Second World War, my dad's job in the Army was to find deserters, and when he found them he ran off with them. I think that when Daddy passed away after being attacked by a hamster, Mother couldn't wait to have him buried because she took his coffin to the cemetery in a sports car.

Mummy didn't like me; she used to sit up for hours with my birth certificate, looking for loopholes. I can still recall when she asked me to leave home. I was three. She'd handed me a trumpet and told me to blow. Then there were the games she insisted on playing with me: Blind-man's buff on Beachy Head ... leap-frog on the M6. Yet she could be kind; so that I wouldn't catch cold in the bath, she'd toss the electric fire in the water. The crunch came when I was kidnapped; the ransom money demanded from Mother for my safe return was only sixpence.... I was with those kidnappers twenty-two years. Eventually they got fed up with me and paid the money themselves.

Not much of a family, but blood is thicker than water. We all need to have ties and roots; I suppose that is why I have all the photographs of my kith and kin.

My musings were interrupted by a faint moan. I looked up, and paled. In a corner, stuffed in the waste-paper basket, was a dying horse. My mind was in a whirl. I was getting in deep with this Velma business and no mistake. I sat up all night with the horse – well, like it or not, I was saddled with it, and a fetlock of good it was doing me.

The vet pronounced the horse dead: H.O.R.S.E.
D.E.A.D. – that's the way he pronounced it. He
reckoned the animal had been poisoned as well as
stabbed, not forgetting the bullet hole in its chest. We
managed to drag it downstairs and I put a 'For Sale' sign
on it. It was the first time I'd flogged a dead horse.

I drew heavily on a cigarette. Just who was the nun?
Why was she stalking me? Was it she who'd killed the
nag? Was Mussels happy with the tramp?

The latter question was soon resolved as Mussels
lumbered into the office. He put the lumber down and
asked me if I'd got a log book. I was in no mood for
games and my face remained wooden. Mussels started
sobbing his heart out. The tramp had rejected the big
man's proposal of marriage and had then exposed
himself to a lapsed vicar. The tramp was now in the
hands of the Social Security; they wanted him to be MC
at their staff dance.

I managed to get rid of Mussels with a promise to play
bingo with him, and to keep the big lug happy, I sang
'Moon River' in a duet with him as he left the office.

I glanced through a pile of bills. It came as a shock to
realize I was so far behind with the rent for the office,
the arrears were ticked off in the Domesday Book. The
silence was broken by the shrill squawk of the phone.
When I answered it, a muffled voice said, 'Stop looking
for Velma if you know what's good for you.'

Anger rose in my craw. 'Oh, and what is good for
me?' I snarled.

'A life of self-denial and a fish diet,' the muffled voice
replied.

It dawned on me who the muffled voice belonged to –
It belonged to Mr Muffle. He was a two-bit crook
who'd had once been a jockey with the Gas Board.
Nowadays he hung around the streets picking pockets
and acting as pimp for a masked pigmy.

I banged the receiver down. Just what the hell was
afoot? Of course, twelve inches, I remembered.

This Velma business was getting me down and no
mistake; my eyes were playing tricks with me. I thought
someone was sitting in my chair – just then a smell of
perfume wafted in my direction. Someone *was* sitting in
my chair in the shadows. Funny, I was sitting in that
chair – who the hell was it on my knee?

'Marlowe,' a sensuous voice whispered in my ear, 'I
want to hire you.'

I nodded and told her how to hire me – just turn the
screw under the chair, that would higher me up six
inches. Hot lips searched out mine and her hands started
fooling around. I pushed her away and swung the
cannon in her direction. 'Okay, baby,' I grunted, 'what's
your name?' Well, we played something for an hour,
and from now on, cricket's had it.

'Find Karl Jerome,' she said quietly. I couldn't see her
face properly ... she was wearing a set of theatrical
whiskers and a false blue nose. 'I like your office,
Marlowe,' she said. 'Did you decorate yourself?'

I shook my head. 'No, lady, I put it on the walls.'

I sensed that she nodded. 'Have you got dry rot?' she
said.

I replied, 'No, it's just the way my shirt's been ironed.'

She walked over to the door with a swaying motion; it

was the first time I'd seen that door sway. 'Be seein' you, Marlowe,' she said, and did a quick impression of a giraffe up a tree before throwing me ten pounds in ten-pence pieces.

I wanted to know more about my mysterious visitor, but although I followed her out into the corridor, she'd vanished. All that was left of her was the heady smell of her perfume and an abandoned Morris Minor.

Karl Jerome ... I racked my memory. Of course! He was reputed to be one of the richest men in town. Frankly, I couldn't see any connection between Velma and Jerome. He was a pillar of society, married to Miriam, née Cockbottom (she'd had two sisters but they died of embarrassment). His father, Jack, had made millions out of tin. He couldn't spend the money because it was made of tin.

This case was getting out of hand, so I put it on the floor. It wasn't mine anyway, my mysterious visitor must have left it.

I opened the case. It was full of ten-pence pieces and a recently stuffed goat. Underneath its tail was a photo-graph of Al Jolson singing 'Mammy' in a nudist camp. I found a sheaf of letters which I placed in my pocket to read later. I was just about to shut the case when I heard a movement behind me. I half turned, but too late; something crashed against my right temple and I fell into a black pit.

I surfaced with a blinding headache and tottered to my feet. The case had gone and my office had been ransacked. Someone had run off with my sacks.

I got out of the office fast. I needed a drink to clear the lances probing in my skull. I found myself sitting in a bar two blocks away. It was called 'Twiggy's Chest' because the beer was flat and warm. I sat there with my large gin — my fourth, I might add, and I can add — six and eight . . . fourteen.

I must have drunk a lot in that bar because I recall falling off my stool and missing the floor.

I woke up the following morning with a mouth that tasted like the lining of a hyena's bowel. I had a splitting headache, it was four a.m. — the alarm was going off — and I was partly in bed with a fat reindeer. I knew something was wrong: I never set the alarm for four.

I read the morning newspapers and showered and the papers got soaked.

I made myself beans on toast, then spent an hour scraping the beans out of the toaster. How did I do it? Well, the answer, my friend, is blowing in the wind.

I arrived in my office and found a tall, slim, grey-haired man waiting for me. Straightaway I knew I was looking at Mr Karl Jerome. I recognized his photograph from the society columns; he went around with the Upper Set — the bottom set he kept in a box.

'Mr Marlowe?' he said softly. 'Forgive me for being so early but I simply had to see you.' I realized that he was a trifle effeminate by his accent, his bearing, his high heels and wedding dress. 'I have a job for you and I'm prepared to pay you well for it.' With that remark, he handed me a hundred pounds in ten-pence pieces on a shovel.

'What's the job?' I growled, and lit a cigarette.

He was silent for a minute as he played a lament on a euphonium; it was a haunting theme, and I played a few bars of it myself on my piccolo.

He told me what the job was as we danced the hornpipe together. It was a simple job. He wanted me to act as his bodyguard that night. He was meeting three men who had a string of pearls for sale, pearls so expensive they were still in the oyster. My task was to make sure there was no funny business, so I decided not to wear my clown's outfit. If the men didn't give him the oyster, I'd winkle them out. No problem, where there's a whelk there's a way. Besides, it would take my mind off Mussels. It never once dawned on me that I would be a prawn in the game.

I agreed to see him later at his villa, and he shook my hand and gave me a slice of wedding cake.

I drove up the winding road that led to his cliff-top villa. It was a beautiful night. The stars twinkled saucily, the sea below boomed out a welcome, and in a thicket a Druid was exposing himself to a bull terrier.

The villa loomed before me, a huge white building that reeked of money. As a precaution, I had disguised myself as King Arthur – it was just as well, for as I opened the iron gates and clanked towards the front door, a Rottweiler dashed out and bit my leg. Luckily, the armour broke all its teeth and I carried on, leaving the animal to pick the bits up with its paw.

Jerome opened the door in his wedding dress (what it

was doing on the door I'll never know). He was dressed as a Cornish Floral Dancer.

We drove off back down the winding road and saw the bull terrier exposing itself to the Druid.

Jerome indicated that we'd arrived at the spot where he was to meet the men with the pearls. I motioned him to stay in the car whilst I had a look around. Something heavy crashed against my temple, and once again I went into a black pit.

Fortunately, my plumed helmet took most of the blow and I staggered to my feet to find a heavily veiled woman holding a pistol in my direction. 'Don't move, Buster,' she said grimly. 'I've got ten bullets in this gun, and I came third at Bisley.'

I sniggered and retorted, 'Big deal, baby, I came second at Bisley.'

She smiled and said sarcastically, 'Well, well, little man, you've had a Bisley day.'

Suddenly I saw a pair of feet sticking out from beneath a bush. I knew it was the body of Karl Jerome because his head was jammed in his euphonium. When I looked around again, the heavily veiled woman had gone, but the Druid and the bull terrier were now exposing themselves to me.

I couldn't leave things like this, so I loaded Jerome's body in the car and drove off to the police station.

The cops grilled me all night then decided to grill bacon instead. 'Listen to me, Marlowe,' said Mike Mallet, 'you are in big trouble. I don't believe a word of your cock-and-bull story.'

In vain I tried to tell him that it wasn't a cock and bull

story, it was a Druid and a bull terrier story, but he would have none of it. Eventually he said I could go.

As I clanked out of the interrogation room, he snarled, 'Mussels Malloy, the big guy – he was arrested last night but knocked out three of my uniformed men, six detectives, two members of an all steel band and Vera Lynn's agent.... I'm gonna get him ... and you too, Marlowe, I swear it.'

I got back to my office, my thoughts in a whirl. All I could think about was whirls. Just what the hell was going on? What connection had Jerome had with the veiled woman? Had she killed him? Was his euphonium playing that bad? Somehow I had an uneasy feeling that Mussels Malloy was tied into all this.... I gave up mulling it all over and watched 'Crossroads' instead.

I rented a wheelbarrow and spent an hour shifting the piles of ten-pence pieces into the other room. When that was finished, I sat down and examined the inside of Jerome's euphonium.... No wonder his playing was crap: inside it, I found a leather cigarette case with five Russian gold-filtered cigarettes in it. What made me do it I'll never know, but I had a hunch – I've had a hunch for years, that's why I walk the way I do. Carefully I unfastened one of the gold filters and out dropped a rolled-up calling card. The writing on it was faint so I put my glasses on (I don't use them all the time, I only need them for seeing, and they are cheaper than a guide dog). The writing sprang into focus: 'Emery Vance, Psychic Consultant, 87 Park View Mansions.'

Nothing made sense. I sat and pondered idly until the phone jerked me back to the present with its shrill jangle that makes my nerves jingle every time it jangles.

The call was from a very irate Mallet. 'Marlowe? You never mentioned the lady with you when Jerome was knocked off.' He sounded quite put out.

'Believe me, Mallet, I didn't want to involve her. Although I don't know who she is, something tells me she's a classy dame,' I said gently.

There was a silence, then Mallet spoke. 'Okay, Marlowe, this time you're off the hook. She *is* a classy dame with a lot of connections in high places, and she's the daughter of a friend of mine.' With that, he rang off.

It was obvious she'd been in touch with the police, but why? I made my mind up to visit Emery Vance. My hunch was strong until I took the coathanger out of my jacket.

Park View Mansions had been a fashionable address once; now it was run down and seedy, and Number 87 was the seediest one in the block. I rang the bell, and the badly chipped door was opened by a Red Indian in full ceremonial dress. His arms were folded and so were his legs. I said, 'How,' and he replied, 'I put one leg under the other.'

'Tell Mr Vance that Philip Marlowe, private investigator, is here to see him.' The Indian indicated that I should come inside and wait in the hall whilst he went to see if Vance would see me. The hallway was full of stuff. . . . Two polecats were on the wall in a glass case;

SKETCH OF PARK VIEW
MANSIONS

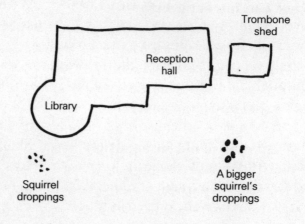

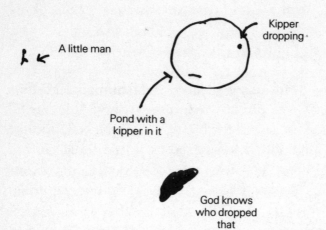

they weren't mounted, they were just shaking hands. My critical, trained gaze took in a sprawl of expensive carpet, rich wallpaper adorning the walls and maroon velvet curtains at the high window.

The hall smelt of incense, and I distinctly heard the sound of somebody chanting an ancient rite. I'd heard that chant once before in Pontin's during a Peruvian Pie Festival in aid of orphans over forty ... those words still sent a chill down my spine:

'There was an old farmer from Greece
Who did terrible things to his geese;
He went too far with a budgie he had
And his parrot phoned the police.'

The Red Indian returned and bade me follow him. I did as instructed, and we walked through a long corridor and into a vast room, where, seated at a dimly lit desk, was Mr Emery Vance. He rose to his feet, a tall, heavily built man wearing a turban and a kilt. 'Will you join me in a glass of sherry?' he said.

I shook my head. 'I'd like to but there wouldn't be enough room in it for two of us.'

He shrugged his thick-set shoulders and started rolling a cigar. He rolled it all over the floor and into the corridor. He came back an hour later in time to catch me going through his drawers, which he was wearing at the time. I sneered, 'You're a phoney, pal – no real Scotsman wears drawers under his kilt.'

He glared at me and spat, 'State your business and get out.'

I leaned over the desk and whispered, 'I found your address in a Russian cigarette that belonged to Karl Jerome, the tin millionaire. I think he was a fence for jewel thieves and I also think, pally, that you're involved as well. By the way, Jerome is dead.'

He must have pressed a button somewhere because the Red Indian glided into the room and grabbed me from behind. Vance came close to me and I lashed out with my foot.

'Blast you!' he gasped. 'I have a crystal ball!'

I shouted back, 'Then you should have known what I was going to do.'

He dropped his kilt and removed the glass splinters. 'You'll pay for that, Marlowe, these balls are fifteen pounds a dozen.'

The Red Indian dragged me down into a chair. Bravely I yelled, 'Listen, Indian, you're nothing to Crow about, let me go or I'll Sioux.' He laughed and asked if he could use that line in his cabaret act.

Emery Vance stood over me and started playing 'Amazing Grace' on a set of bagpipes. The dreadful noise went through me. 'STOP IT, DAMN YOU!' I screamed.

'Certainly, Marlowe, just tell me where the other cigarettes are.'

I had to stall for time ... because the stall wasn't ready to open. 'The other cigarettes are in my office.'

He said, 'I don't believe you, flatfoot,' and began to play 'Yellow Submarine' on the infernal instrument. It was too much. I blacked out.

Chapter Two

'She was a Class dame with a great Form and you couldn't Teacher anything.

I was really Cane on her but I didn't seem to Mortar to her and she got Board.

Things came to a Head when I tried to Chalk to her. "Why won't you Lesson to me?" I cried, but I wasn't on the right Lines. I knew I'd never Master her. She was going out with a guy called Gym and he was really on the Ball.

I knew I'd never come to Terms with her and I started taking Prep pills ... and that just about Sums it up.'

Marlowe

Somebody splashed cold water on my face and I spluttered to life. Vance was standing by the window ignoring me, and two hefty guys with local cop written all over them were going through my pockets.

'Okay, pal, come clean,' one of the hefty guys said, and he handed me a loofah and a basin.

I leapt from my chair and lunged at one of the two men. I caught him with a left hook to the chin and a right hook to the stomach. He caught me with a right cross and a left upper-cut to the jaw. I got him with a left jab and a right to the solar plexus. He caught me with another upper-cut and a punch to the ribs, but I got him on the chin with a right jab. Vance stopped the fight by hitting me over the head with a stone elephant, which was unfair because I was ahead on points. I've always had points on my head.

'Take him away,' Vance said wearily, and the two men took me into the hall and weighed me. Fourteen stone eight pounds. It saddened me; once I'd had broad shoulders and a deep chest, but that was all behind me now.

Outside Park View Mansions, I was released by the two guys. 'What I can't figure,' I gasped, 'is what two local cops are doing here?'

One of them put his face close to mine. 'Mind you keep away, buddy, from now on,' he grated.

I looked down at the gravel drive, and saw a pile of feathers. 'Where's the Red Indian?' I wanted to know.

'Oh, him? He's over there.'

I looked in the direction he was pointing. The Indian was lying on his back with about two hundred arrows stuck in him. It was quite apparent that he'd died of woodworm. Before I could ask why they'd killed him, one of them hit me with the butt of a gun on my temple and I dived once more into a black pit.

I surfaced to consciousness in a room that seemed full of smoke. Feebly I tried to shout, 'Fire!' but no sound came

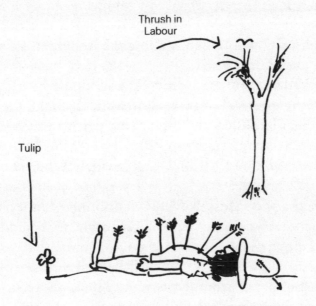

Police sketch of dead Red Indian on lawn. Thought to be a Blackfoot but his neck was same colour. Note grouping of arrows – nobody claimed the first prize – a Noddy trilby.

out of my mouth.... My head was full of cotton wool, and I knew I'd been drugged. I managed to heave myself off the bed I was lying on and fell to the floor.... I attempted to crawl to the door but it was a million miles away. I drummed my heels and croaked again.

This time the door opened and a man in a white jacket came in. 'What's the matter, punk?' he snarled, and took me by the collar and dragged me back on the bed. Through a swirling mist, I saw him pull out a syringe which he stabbed into my arm.

'No, no ... not that ... anything but that,' I whispered.

'Anything?' he replied, pulling his underpants down. 'What about this then?'

I looked at it and whispered, 'The syringe, the syringe!'

Dreams came ... strange dreams. I could see my father again holding me in his arms when I was a baby, and he was saying to my mother, 'I don't know what to make of him,' and Mother was saying, 'What about a rug?'

I dreamt that Mussels Malloy and Emery Vance were chasing the bald nun with a crocodile that suddenly turned into a pair of shoes. I was going nuts.

Somehow I swung myself off the bed and started to walk around and around the room. I had to force myself to keep going, my legs were mere strips of rubber and the smoke in my head was getting thicker.

How long it took before my brain began to clear I don't know, but clear it did and I took deep breaths of air to fill my aching lungs and rid them of the poison that had so weakened me. I had to get out, and quickly. I needed a weapon, but what? I looked under the bed and found a chamber pot. There was some lettering on it in German, so it must have been an authentic Jerry.

I secreted myself behind the door and yelled out, 'I think the Poll Tax is a good idea!'

That did it. The man in the white coat rushed in carrying a bazooka and a wax model of Neil Kinnock.

I hit him on the back of his head with the chamber pot. It did the trick, but I wished I'd emptied it first. I stepped over his inert body and ran out.

There was no sign of anyone around. I crept down the stairs and into the street, totally forgetting the fact that I was naked except for my fedora and ankle socks.

I was lucky, the street was empty apart from a blind beggar playing a mouth organ. I talked him into letting me have his clothes in exchange for filling in his VAT return, grabbed a cab, and shot away.

Something was preying at the back of my mind. I recalled being carried into the room I'd just escaped from; I was still aware of things, and I remember seeing a man lying on a bed in another room ... a big man, a very big man — Mussels Malloy.

I gave the cab driver his fare from the money on the beggar's tray and hared up the flight of stairs to my office. I had to think. It was a good job I did — this wasn't my office. Where the hell was I? I shook my head and looked out of the window. It wasn't my town either.

There was nothing for it. I would have to retrace my steps to where I'd been imprisoned. I had no choice.

Just then, as if fate had intervened, the taxi driver came into the strange office. He was scowling. 'In the money you gave me there were six buttons and a Polo mint.'

I could have hugged him. Searching though the office filing cabinet I found a five-pound note and a pamphlet on constipation and asked the driver to take me back to the place he'd picked me up. He scratched his head. 'Oh yeah, I remember. The Clinic,' he said.

As we weaved through the traffic I tried to make sense

of what had happened to me. The cabbie pulled up
outside the Clinic. He only wanted the pamphlet on
constipation but I bought the buttons back off him for a
quid.

There was no movement inside the Clinic. I tiptoed
along a corridor very quietly. The noise of a typewriter
drew me towards a room and I saw an elderly man at a
desk, typing. At my entrance he looked up and went
pale, and made to reach into a drawer. I slammed the
drawer on his fingers; it would be a long time before he
drew again.

There was a gun in the drawer. I grabbed it and
shoved the muzzle into his white coat. 'Okay, my friend,
I want some answers and fast. Let's start with you, then
tell me where I am,' I said menacingly.

DR SCHMEKEL. Born in Budapest in a drought.
Studied dentistry and crocodile midwifery for a man in a
mess. Played snooker with cucumber for charity and
prone to warts if left out to dry. Wanted in Peru for
cheating at Cluedo and showing his bottom to an
unstable Mormon.

He trembled. 'Really, sir, you shouldn't be out of bed ... you're still under medication.'

'Medication my arse,' I said.

He shook his balding head. 'No, sir, we gave you the medication in your arm.'

I slapped him around and out tumbled the story. His name was Doctor Franz Von Schmekel, and I had been taken to the Clinic, suffering from narcotic poisoning, by the local cops, the two hefty guys I'd met earlier. I sure remembered them. The town I was in was called Miresea-on-the-Crouch, a small town, so small, in fact, the speed limit signs were back to back.

I felt myself going giddy and the good doctor looked at me with concern. 'Why don't you sit down and give me that gun?' he said smoothly, his voice like treacle.

Grimly I shook my head and the mists went away. 'No dice, doctor,' I said, so there was no chance to play a game of Monopoly. He paled again when I asked him to open his safe. I needed cash to get out of this burg. He meekly complied. Inside the safe were two hundred pounds in ten-pence pieces. I loaded my pockets with as much as I could carry, then, just as I was about to go, I saw an address scrawled on a notepad. There was something else ... the smell of a perfume that I remembered from the night Karl Jerome was murdered. I put two and two together....

I found the place without too much difficulty. The neighbourhood was middle class and the address turned out to be a large bungalow in well-manicured gardens. I rang a brass bell and when the door opened I gazed at one of the most beautiful women I have ever seen.

'Miss Lola Vallance?' I said politely.

She grinned at me. 'Cut the crap, Marlowe. Just how the hell did you find me?' She beckoned me inside. She had hips that swayed like two kids fighting in a tent. She stopped and shouted, 'Get out, you sons of bitches!' and two kids ran from under her skirt. 'Kids, hey Marlowe?' she breathed seductively.

'I like kids,' I said in jocular mood. 'I used to go to school with them.'

She smiled a forced smile then spoilt it by saying that it was a rotten joke. She patted the cushion on the settee and I sat next to her.

What a doll – her legs were longer than the M6 and the curve of her breasts excited me. Her eyes were limpid pools of blue innocence, and even when she broke wind it didn't seem out of place, although I had to open the windows.

Her name wasn't her real one. She was actually christened Ethel Grubb and she was originally from Oldham. . . . Now that struck a chord. I took a shot at it, the cord broke and the curtains fell down.

'Quit clowning around, Marlowe,' she said angrily, and threw a bag of Patna rice at me.

I lost my temper. I picked up a cavalry sabre off the table and lunged at her. She retaliated by striking me with a pot-glazed gnome and I had to duck as she followed up the attack with a crossbow. Wildly I looked around for a weapon, and fortunately in the fireplace I saw a hand-grenade. It exploded and blew her eyebrows off. Boy, was she mad! With a yell she rushed at me with a rocket launcher strapped to her back, and a missile streaked past my ear.

Suddenly we were in each other's arms, fighting with daggers, but then our lips met in a passionate welding and we fell back on to the settee, ripping each other's clothes off. Our love-making was violent and our mutual climax was like the crashing of the sea on the shore. After it was over we smoked a pipe – we'd run out of cigarettes – and got dressed. We laughed when we realized that we'd put the wrong clothes back on. She looked cute in my worn blue serge and I felt at home in her bra and pantyhose.

'Lola,' I said tenderly, ' "Lucky", the guy who owned the casino in Oldham, he was your brother, wasn't he?'

She nodded dumbly and began to cry. The tears ran down her cheeks like a waterfall, and out came the sorry narrative of woe.

Her brother, Arthur 'Lucky' Grubb, had been a well-known archaeologist, famous for having found the hidden tomb of Ram the Elder in the Valley of the Kings. He had ignored the curse which warned, 'He who defiles the sacred tomb of the Mighty Ram will suffer the punishment of dismemberment.' Inside the tomb Grubb discovered a priceless set of pearls hidden in the mummy's jockstrap. Two days later, whilst sitting on a makeshift commode in the desert reading a copy of the

Radio Times which had been cut into squares with string looped through them, his right leg fell off. The curse had worked.

Depressed, he got a job in Cairo making hops for a brewery, until he got too stout and then he became bitter. Having only one leg, he didn't think anyone would want to marry him, but one day he met a woman who swept him off his foot. Her left hand was missing and she had a hook strapped to her wrist. On their honeymoon, a seagull shit in his eye, his wife took the stuff out of his pupil forgetting about the hook, and that's how he came to lose his eye.

His wife never forgave herself and went insane. She began to think she was a Hoover, and would lie for hours on the landing, humming loudly with the cleaning hose rammed up her rectum. They took her away to a mental institution and although she still thought she was a vacuum cleaner, she started to pick up better.

'Lucky' gave up archaeology for good and opened a casino. Ethel changed her name to Lola and sang torch songs to the clients as they gambled, but she gave up the torch songs when the batteries ran out.

It became obvious that 'Lucky' was in trouble. Lola found some letters with coal tar smeared all over them, and realized that he was being blackmailed. It was at the casino that she met Karl Jerome, and she knew he had a hold on her brother – it was a half-nelson. Jerome more or less took over the casino and started putting his own people in. . . . One of them was a girl called Velma.

Some months later, Mussels Malloy came on the scene as a bouncer on the casino door. One night, after

'Lucky' had refused to submit to more blackmail, Jerome had Mussels break his victim's arm and plunge it into a vat of cooling jelly. The arm never set properly and it withered.

'Mussels wouldn't leave Velma alone.... Mind you, she egged the poor slob on – one night she'd poach them, other nights she'd fry them, no wonder his brains were scrambled,' Lola said grimly. 'When Velma left the casino, Malloy went too, and that's the last I saw of either of them.'

The jigsaw was falling into place now; all I needed was a few bits to finish the chimney off and the jigsaw was complete. It was apparent that Lola had wanted to kill Jerome, but I knew now that she hadn't. Then who had?

One thing was for sure, wherever Mussels had been, there had been death as well.

I left Lola Vallance and drove home. The flat was strangely empty, and I knew it lacked a woman's touch. I couldn't get Lola out of my head. What a dame! I fell into a deep sleep. I must have slept like log because when I woke up my head was in the fireplace.

Somebody was banging on my door, and I was sure it was the cops. I was right. Standing on the stoop was Mallet.

'Okay, Marlowe,' he wheezed. 'Let's talk.'

I drew on a cigarette – I forget what I drew, but it looked like a wasp with a big bum. I decided to come clean, so I had a bath whilst Mallet sat on the bidet.

I told him everything as he scrubbed my back, then he

got in the bath and I scrubbed his back. I put my towelling robe on and sat on the bidet, having first put some greasy plates in the bath water for Mallet to play with.

Even to my ears the story I unfolded seemed unreal, but I had the bruises to show for it. As Mallet was blow-drying his wig, he filled me in on the missing pieces. There was a piece missing from the front of his wig and a piece missing from the top of it.

A lot of what he told me, I'd already deduced. Karl Jerome had been a blackmailer and the fence for a big syndicate that dealt in stolen jewels. Jerome had realized just how much 'Lucky's' string of pearls was worth and had tried to buy them off the unfortunate casino owner, but somewhere, he'd got big enemies and now he was no more.

As Mallet fitted his wig back on with some Super-Glue, he jerked his head round and said casually, 'By the way, gumshoe, the two local cops who beat you up are on the force in Miresea-on-the-Crouch, as I think you already know. However, their names are Lauren and Hardie, thought you'd like to know.' With that he slammed the door and was gone.

Like it or not, I had to return to that little town. I wanted to see those two cops ... they were hiding something and I wanted to know what it was.

When I reached Miresea, I checked into a hotel that had seen better days. It was clean right enough: the bed sheets were changed everyday, from one bed to another.

There wasn't a single flea in my bed – they were all married with families. In the bedroom there was rising damp being held at bay by the falling damp. I didn't have a headboard on the bed, just a lifebelt. The dampness was so bad, the furniture had been undersealed. There were mouse droppings everywhere: one mouse doing it, one mouse sweeping it into a heap and another one looking for fresh sites.

The room smelt so bad, I brought a pig in to use as an air freshener. It was such a small bedroom, so tiny, when I turned the light off I was in bed before it was dark.

When I rang for room service, a tennis ball hit me. Eventually I managed to get fish and chips; God knows how long they'd had the fish in stock but it was sucking the vinegar off my chips. The coffee I ordered was awful. I rang down and complained: 'This coffee is like mud,' I said. The manager said, 'I'm not surprised, it was only ground this morning.'

I didn't sleep a wink in that hotel. Something kept rustling in the lavatory and crickets were chirping all night long in the closet.

The view from the window was quite good, with an excellent outlook on the disused minefield that led to the Saxon war graves near the sewage silo.

Miresea was a dump all right. I plugged my electric razor in and the traffic lights went out. The traffic lights, by the way, were so old they were in black and white.

It was bitterly cold in that bedroom, the windows were fogged up on the inside. At the finish I sucked a peppermint and sat round my tongue. The management

MIRESEA-ON-THE-
CROUCH

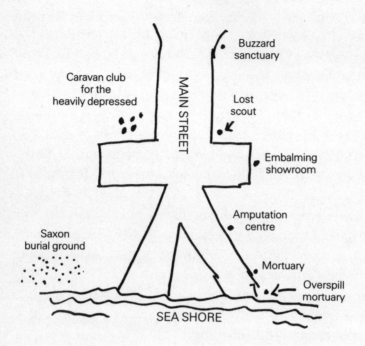

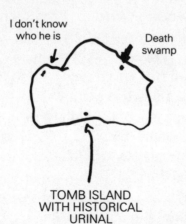

TOMB ISLAND
WITH HISTORICAL
URINAL

was useless: I complained about the intense cold and they sent up a walrus.

I was glad when morning came and the porter helped me to get dressed with a blowlamp. It was too late for the walrus, the poor sod had frozen to death licking its own blubber. What really annoyed me was they tried to charge me extra for eating the mushrooms off the wall.

I entered the police station and demanded to see the Superintendent, who turned out to be a fat man with a six-inch long moustache. I walked into his office (because that's where he was so there was no point in going anywhere else) and I smiled brightly and said, 'Hello, Super,' and he looked up and replied, 'Hello, wonderful.' It was odd watching him steam-ironing his moustache, and it made conversation difficult.

'I would like to see Lauren and Hardie,' I said sternly.

The Superintendent shook his head and steam hissed from the iron. 'No can do, boy,' he muttered. 'They're on a stake-out.'

I glanced out of the window and saw them carrying a steak from a butcher's shop. I bristled. 'Listen, call them in, and do it now.'

He grunted but rose to his feet and poked his head through the window. 'Lauren? Hardie? Get your asses up here, pronto.'

The faces of the two men when they saw me were a picture, and I knew they'd recognized me. I made them talk plenty, and soon I knew all there was to know about the goings on both at 87 Park View Mansions and at the Clinic in Miresea.

It was simple enough. Emery Vance rented off rooms to mobsters on the run, hence Mussels Malloy's presence in the Clinic the other night. In his role as a so-called psychic he wheedled money out of rich old women who were anxious to get in touch with loved ones beyond the grave. It was a sweet racket but he was greedy for more. I knew that my next step would put one foot in front of the other, and I wanted to see Vance.

I left Lauren and Hardie with the Superintendent, and those two boys were really shaken up. They'd been taking money from Vance for turning a blind eye to the goings-on there, plus free palm readings as well.

But I was far from solving the murders and finding the killer, and I was still under suspicion by the cops.

There was excitement in Miresea that afternoon: they'd found someone alive in a bus shelter, and free pancakes were being tossed in a billiard hall.

At the clinic there was no sign of Emery Vance, but the dead Red Indian was still there. He was now a photographic model for Japanese tourists.

I went back to the rotten hotel. Even in the daytime it was still rotten. A message, relayed from my office, was waiting for me. It was from somebody called Mrs Fettersfill. The address wasn't too far away, in fact nothing was very far away in Miresea ... the council took it in when it rained.

Mrs Fettersfill lived in a house so old the mice wore powdered wigs and the light fittings were thatched. I didn't get to speak with her, mainly because she was

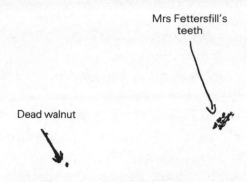

Mrs Fettersfill's
teeth

Dead walnut

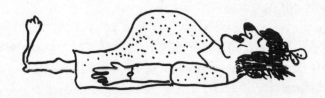

Position of Mrs Fettersfill when I found her body. A policeman with a nephew in Ealing said he discovered the corpse glued to a ladder upstairs in a banana orchard. Who moved the body? Must interview the masked sailor who sat knitting collars for apricots.

very dead. Her neck had been broken in such a way it must have taken someone with enormous strength to do it. It was broken in three places: bathroom, kitchen and attic. By the side of the telephone I espied a notepad on which was written in pencil, 'On ARQ ... V?' That was all.

I phoned the local police and got out of that house

fast. It was clear that Mussels Malloy had killed the old woman, but why? Nothing made any sense, and mentally I went through the whole business again and again as I drove back to the city in a rented car ...

Mussels Malloy, Emery Vance, the missing Velma, the bald nun, Lauren and Hardie, Lola's brother 'Lucky', Karl Jerome and Doctor Schmekel ... or would you rather be a mule? I shook my head and concentrated on the traffic flow. To take my mind off things I switched on the radio. Sweet music wafted out, a pleasant song by a rock group called 'Snot Raggs and His Crushers'. The song title was, 'Beat Me, Daddy, to a Battered Pulp'.

At the end of the song a mellow voice said, 'Have a nice day, yo'all, this is Freddy from ARQ station wishin' yo'all the big bye-bye.' I pulled the car over on to the hard shoulder. ARQ ... V?

I found a telephone kiosk that hadn't been vandalized and rang directory inquiries. ARQ, a soft voice informed me, was the local radio station in Miresea. I got back into the car, spun the machine around and returned to Dumpsville.

There was no trouble in finding the station, it was in a garden shed next door to the Rotten Hotel.

I spoke to Freddy, a hyped-up kinda guy in a track suit and gold chains wrapped round his neck. I slipped him twenty pounds in ten-pence pieces and he agreed to look through the discs he'd played in the last two days. We nearly deafened ourselves with the records; it was no wonder kids were going Mutt and Jeff. My hunch paid off. Freddy pulled the handle on my vest and three bells came up. From the old record on the turntable came a sexy torch singer's voice. Freddy stopped the turntable, I looked at the sleeve. Bingo – just one name on it – Velma.

That was the reason Mrs Fettersfill was no longer with us, but how had Mussels got to know about her discovery?

I was tired but no way did I intend to stay another night in Miresea-on-the-Crouch. I decided to drive back to my flat. On the freeway going back I glanced in the mirror. A long black saloon was following me.

I tried to shake the pursuing car off but its front bumper was jammed on my rear bumper. We travelled along for about six miles in that ridiculous position, until a police motorcycle waved us down.

As I leapt from my car, the driver of the one following me also got out, opened the boot, took out a horse and galloped away across a field full of cows. It was the bald nun again. I got rid of the speed cop by bribing him with five pounds in ten-pence pieces and ran across the field after the horse, which had unseated its rider after falling into a bog. It was then that I suspected for a brief moment that the nun was German, because I heard her shouting as she weaved through the cows, 'Ach Dung ... Ach Dung.'

I lost her in a clump of trees. On the way back through the herd of cows my hat dropped off and I tried on four before I realized they were cow pats. I knelt by the side of a small stream and washed the cow shit off my head. As I did so, I saw a bull with a broken neck lying in the branches of a tree.... So, Mussels had been here as well. I couldn't figure it out: was he after the bald nun, or *was he* the bald nun?

I recalled something my Albanian governess had once said to me: 'Fychia naikla colpoi.' I never knew what it meant, but I'd never forgotten it.

It was dark when I reached the city ... my city. A sprawling mass of neon glare and concrete towers leaning over litter-pitted streets that retched pools of pale illumination from ragged blocks of tenements. And somewhere in my city was a murderer.

As soon as I opened the door, I knew that somebody had been in my flat. I could smell that elusive perfume that I'd smelt somewhere before as well as a strong pong of disinfectant, and I realized that my daily help had cleaned up the mess the cat had done again.

Somebody knew of my movements, but who? I decided to set a trap. I plucked hairs from my head and with Sellotape, stuck them across every door from lock to jamb. If anyone else came in whilst I was out, I'd know.

I left the apartment and walked into a bar, which hurt because it was an iron bar. I drank alone, lost in my thoughts. Suddenly there was a tap on my shoulder. I turned to see who had invaded my privacy. I wished I hadn't. . . . It was Mussels Malloy.

He didn't speak, he simply tucked me under his arm and off we went into the street. I don't know how far we walked but someone asked Mussels for his passport.

At last, after climbing a flight of stairs, Mussels threw

me into a chair in a dirty room ... and it was a dirty room. There were so many cobwebs about the furniture looked as if it had been back-combed. The carpet was so filthy, beetles were walking across it in surgical boots, and mice were throwing themselves on the trap.

'Okay, Marlowe,' the giant rasped. 'Why ain't you found my Velma? Cute as lace panties, my Velma. Youse let me down, punk.'

He placed his massive arms around my waist and started to squash my rib-cage into powder. I gasped for air and beat a tattoo on his nose with my fist. It was useless. I was fighting for breath. I remembered that I had once bought a fountain pen that spurted out a lethal gas when you depressed the top of it. After folding me in half over the radiator, he threw me up to the ceiling, and as I came down, got me in a Boston Crab. This was my chance. I pulled out the fountain pen, depressed the top – and ink came out. There was only one thing left to do. I wrote 'Help' on his forehead.

'Stop, you big ape!' I yelled as he put a reef knot in my spine. To my surprise, he did just that, then started to sob his heart out.

'Why oh why did you call me a big ape, Marlowe?' he said chokingly.

I couldn't believe it. He slumped on the floor, his head in his arms. I squirted some three-in-one oil up my leg and released my head from under my ankles, and with my teeth unfastened the knots in my arms. I snapped. 'Big ape.... Big ape!' I screamed at him, and he moaned in utter despair. 'Just who the hell do you think you are, hey?'

He rolled on his back and asked me to tickle his tummy. That was enough for me. I gave him a bunch of bananas and ran out. I didn't know where I was and I staggered for mile after mile until I found my bearings, then I phoned Mallet and told him what had happened. I gave him a rough guide as to where he'd find Mussels. I'd had it with that moron, the man was a lunatic, and a dangerous one at that.

None of the hairs on my doors was broken when I examined them after getting back to my flat, yet my apartment was in a mess. Someone had been in again, but what the hell were they looking for?

I slept fitfully, and my daily help woke me up with a welcome cup of tea. Annie had only been with me a short while; my old cleaning woman accidentally took an overdose of Alka Seltzer and fizzed to death. Annie looked about sixty on a good day, her hair was all matted and she had a faint beard, but she looked after me very well. I drank my tea and ten minutes later she gave me breakfast in bed. It slid off the plate when she threw it, but I didn't mind. There's something erotic about a poached egg on quilt. I knew why she was annoyed – I'd spilt some tea down her frilly lace-edged pinafore. It served me right for wearing it.

There was nothing in the morning mail, just a letter from the funeral parlour saying that if I didn't pay the last instalment on my uncle's burial, up he'd come.

It was mid morning when I got to the office, and the letter from the funeral parlour jogged my memory. I'd agreed to attend the cremation of Karl Jerome at twelve-thirty p.m. I looked at my watch. I'd never make it in time, so I rang the crematorium and they said that they'd keep him on a low light until I got there.

There was a small knot of mourners when I arrived at the crematorium, plus the police in the shape of Mallet, who nodded to me. Everyone was glad I'd arrived. They were anxious to get on because by now Jerome was getting crisp round the edges.

I didn't recognize many people at the crematorium; there were a lot of women present but they were heavily veiled. There were some tough-looking men wearing Foster Grants and chewing gum in the background, but I saw no sign of Mussels Malloy or Doctor Schmekel. One lady in black with a dark veil crept into the foreground, and there was something about her stance that I thought I recognized. After all, it isn't often that somebody does a cartwheel at a funeral. I shuffled forward to have a closer peek as she took a bow, but a cart selling tripe and cow-heel got in the way.

Somebody was passing a hat round for the Liverpool gospel singer in a frogman's suit, when I sighted three chefs in the same pair of trousers taking the frogman's suit off the hat being passed around. At that moment I sensed an element of farce had crept in. I cried out with a terrible wrath, 'In the name of God, cease this carnival! A man has just been incinerated; what was once a living, pulsing human being is now white ash.

'No matter how he conducted himself through this vale of tears, he is by the very code of morality entitled to respect in his demise. What gives you the right to wax in such a lunatic fashion at this, his final chapter?

'As my old Albanian governess used to say during Lent, "Fychia naikia colpoi" ... can we not be humble on such a day? Remember these words, oh jesting sinners: it's not the size that attracts the flies, it's the gyppo round the rim.

'Open your hearts and think only good things, let not animosity cloud thy natural purity.'

I paused for breath and somebody shouted, 'Bollocks!'

I was in a towering rage, and I had to calm down otherwise I would have fallen off the tower. 'Oh, the bastards,' I murmured as I chewed a sliver of tripe.

Silently I weaved through the stones of forgotten people and clambered into my car. I hate funerals ... they are so final, somehow.

Suddenly, through a wreath of cigarette smoke that I'd idly blown, I saw 'Piggy' Valdez, a two-bit pimp, in deep conversation with a nun. I braked the auto, and idly blew a wreath of smoke through that cigarette. Covertly I watched them, and the cigarette blew smoke idly in that wreath. I couldn't figure it but I knew what I saw meant something, and again I blew a wreath of cigarettes in idle smoke through that.

'Piggy' walked quickly away from the nun and I followed her in my third gear: cardigan, shorts and plimsolls.

Just what would a low-life type want with a nun? Unless, the lady was none other than the mysterious bald nun! That thought snapped me into a state of alertness and I concentrated on following her, which was difficult because I was in the car, of course, and she was walking through Marks and Spencer's.

Getting up the moving staircase was the worst thing for me; my aerial snapped when it snagged in a woman's earring and my left front tyre flattened an exhibition of Japanese paper canoes.

The nun was unaware of being followed, and I managed to drive out of the store, release a pensioner trapped under the exhaust, and park on a double yellow line. I was just in time; the nun came out of Marks holding a giant woollen hedgehog and bingo! She was bald. Her wimple had come off and was hanging on the snout of the hedgehog. As she darted away, I flagged down a cab, pulled out my private detective card and cracked on I was a policeman. I commandeered the taxi, firstly giving the bewildered cabbie five pounds in ten-pence pieces and a Polaroid snap of the giant woollen hedgehog.

The bald nun was standing by a set of traffic lights. I braked and said 'May I offer you a lift, Mother? I am a very religious person and help the church all I can.'

She smiled and said how kind it was of me and got in the back of the cab. Before I could ask her where we were going, she pulled out a Bowie knife and started ripping apart the giant woollen hedgehog.

'Keep your eyes on the road, Marlowe,' the nun rasped, and I felt the Bowie knife at my throat. 'What a bum sleuth you turned out to be.'

At her command I drove out of town and into a small deserted banana plantation – and there are not many of those left in Hendon. She ordered me to take my clothes off, then tied me to the taxi's axle with my braces. I watched her take a paper parcel from the hedgehog's belly and examine the contents, which appeared to be a string of pearls ... and now I knew the identity of the bald nun.

'You still can't believe that your son is a killer, can you?' I said gently, as I tried to avoid the drip of oil plopping in between the cleft of my buttocks.

She snarled, 'You know too much, flatfoot,' and kicked me in the rib-cage with her football boots.

I gasped and started to sing 'Moon River.' The nun groaned and joined in the chorus before beginning to sob with grief.

'It's no use, Mrs Malloy,' I whispered. 'Mussels is in big trouble. Where were you when he needed you?'

Her story tumbled out in a torrent of words, and just like her son she was boring. So much so, I booked a week's holiday in Nepal.

When she'd left 'The Martha Haggett Trombone Romany Dwarfs' music-hall act, she had found life dull as a wife and mother to ten children, so she took a job working on an Antarctic whaler. However, she contracted rheumatism in her shoulder and found that she couldn't throw the harpoon properly.

One night, the whaler sank with all hands; she was all right because she was travelling by whale at the time. She was washed ashore on an island where she lived off penguin meat and tandoori take-aways until a ship carrying a troupe of ballet dancers picked her up.

Whilst on the ship she met and fell in love with a young dancer ... Karl Jerome. During the finale of 'The Dying Swan' Jerome confessed that he was a jewel thief and that he wasn't registered for VAT. She had her money sewn up in the hem of her knickers, and after a night of passion in the ship's tool shed, he stole her bloomers and ran off to a post office to open a special account.

Mrs Malloy was devastated; they had been her best drawers, and she lost the will to live. Luckily, a group of nuns found her in a gas oven and took her back to the convent with them. For ten wonderful years she lived in the convent, cleaning and washing for the nuns, and juggling for them when they got fed up. Now and again for a change, she'd sneak out of the convent and gorge

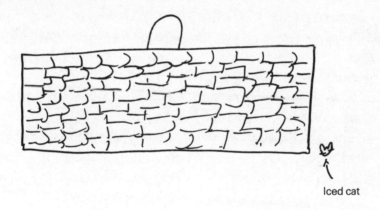

Iced cat

The bald nun walking past a wall. A mistress of disguise with a medal for horse massaging and decorative plumbing. Came third in a flu epidemic. Trained whippets in the convent and fancied Burt Lancaster.

herself on fish and chips. On one such occasion, after she'd eaten the fish and chips, she started reading the newspaper they'd been wrapped up in, and her heart stopped. There was the headline: 'Mussels Malloy Sought in Downtown Slaying of Bank Teller'.

She couldn't believe it – her little boy, that sweet, fourteen-stone baby she'd held in her arms with the help of a crane – her little Mussels – now a criminal, wanted by the police! She refused to accept it. She didn't go back to the convent that night; instead she scoured the bars and back alleys looking for her son.

Dimly she remembered that her boy had known a gypsy who used to make cork freckles in a tannery. She made her way there. The tannery was no more but the building still stood, albeit in a state of disrepair. Gingerly she clambered through a broken window and saw a wan light shining from a shuttered room. She didn't hesitate to open the door. The room was full of unsold boxes of cork freckles, and on a table sat a wizened man sewing pockets on to a turkey.

The man looked up. Mrs Malloy said, 'Are you the gypsy who knew my son, Mussels Malloy?'

The old Romany nodded. 'You must be his mother,' he replied.

Mrs Malloy said she was, and the old gypsy said, 'Can you prove it?'

She sat at his knees and sang 'Moon River' and then whistled 'The Lambeth Walk' in Greek. That satisfied the old man, and he glued a freckle on to her lip.

'I want to see my son,' said Mrs Malloy awkwardly,

because the freckle the man had put on her lip was sliding off.

'I remember you on the halls, Mrs Malloy,' the old man wheezed. 'You were absolutely wonderful in those days. I loved the way you used to do that impression of Mussolini's armpit.'

They talked about the old days for an hour and Mrs Malloy couldn't stop him sticking freckles all over her, so she had to be brusque. 'Let's get back to what I came for. Where is my son?'

The old gypsy said, 'I'm buggered if I know,' and then went to sleep.

Mrs Malloy was livid; she'd never been that colour before and she felt silly. She woke the old Romany up and asked him why he was sewing pockets on a turkey, and he said, 'So that you can stuff them from the outside.' She knew then that he was barmy.

Three days later, Mussels Malloy climbed over the convent wall and he and his mother embraced in her cell. He was so glad to see Mom he kept ruffling her hair and in the morning it had all fallen out. His mummy was bald, but she didn't care; seeing her son was all that mattered. She vowed to look after him, and that was how she had got involved in the case.

I asked her about Velma, but she said she'd never heard of her, and I believed her. What puzzled me about her strange story was how Mussels had known where his mother was. When I asked her that, she went quiet for a moment then blurted out, 'Damn you, Marlowe, the old gypsy told Mussels on an outing to a power station – my boy was always keen on pylons. The gypsy told him how stupid I had looked with those freckles glued on my face ... He laughed when he said it, Marlowe, but he won't laugh again.'

As she spoke the words, I knew that Mussels Malloy must have killed the old gypsy for insulting his mother ... and she knew that I knew what I knew, and I knew my fate was sealed. She dragged me from under the car. I was dripping with oil and axle grease, and she threw her head back and roared with maniacal laughter. I couldn't get free from my bonds, and I was conscious of my nakedness.

'I know what you know, Marlowe. You knew, didn't you, what I knew? So knowing what you know, you know too much, you know that, don't you?' She had an axe in her hands. She slowly lifted it up. I wriggled and squirmed, I even tried singing 'Moon River' in Yiddish, but to no avail. She was going to kill me.... I was about to be axed from another job.

I screamed aloud. Fear opened my bowels with a trumpet solo and I closed my eyes. I waited for the first chop. And waited. Nothing happened. I opened one eye, and saw Ma Mussels lying on the ground, holding her nose. I heard her pant, 'Bloody hell, lad, what have you had to eat?' With that, she passed out cold. I wriggled over to where the axe lay and swiftly managed to saw through the bonds holding my wrists. I was free. I didn't hang about. I bounded away like a startled gazelle and

left that old twit on the ground shouting, 'Pooh....
Pooh!' More by luck than good judgement, I chanced
upon a fairly busy road and hitched a lift on a lorry
carrying conduit to Dorking, which surprised me,
because I thought it would have gone by tube. I
mentioned that little pun to the lorry driver and he
called me something under his breath.

I was exhausted when I got home to the apartment.
Thankfully old Annie was still there and she drew me a
hot bath. I sank into it blissfully.

Annie was full of good old-fashioned concern when
she heard of my not inconsiderable adventure, and she
ushered me off to bed with a glass of hot milk. I slept
and slept....

I awoke as fresh as the proverbial daisy, made a light
breakfast and cantered off to the office.

Mike Mallet was waiting for me and his face was
grim.

'Hi, Mike.' I said. He didn't reply; instead his lips
tightened even more. I stared at him, an uneasy feeling
creasing my gut. Something was terribly wrong, I'd
never seen him chew his feet before, at least not without
a salad dressing.

'I'll tell you what's biting me – this,' he said, and
handed me a squashed bee.

'Mike, we've known each other long enough to
confide in each other,' I said quietly, as he picked
strands of his sock from a molar.

'I'll tell you, Marlowe,' he hissed. 'The Commissioner is on my tail about the murders in this goddamn city. He wants results.'

I gave him three results, two of them from the second divison.

He wasn't amused. 'Listen to me, wise guy,' he yelled. 'You'd better come clean or your ass will be on the line. I mean it, Marlowe.' When his anger had subsided, he told me that the body of an old gypsy had been found in a disused tannery, sewn inside a turkey.... A shiver yo-yoed up my back.

'The old guy was discovered by an FBI undercover agent posing as an unfrocked Jesuit to break up a spy ring for a lettuce grower. He found the body tightly sewn up in the turkey, only the old man's leg sticking down from the parson's nose made him suspect that something was wrong.' Mallet paused and glared at me. 'The old gypsy had been murdered by having a large amount of stuffing rammed down his gullet.'

Before I could say anything, Mallet went on, 'Then we get a report that the body of a bald nun has been found with an axe through her head, and do you know something, Marlowe?' he said in a grating voice. 'That's exactly what we found.'

There comes a time in the life of a private eye when the truth must be told. This whole damn business was so screwy, I had to spill everything I knew to Mallet.

Once before, three years ago, I'd faced a situation like this one.... New York, the Farrington Affair.

Saul Farrington, a wealthy tortoise breeder and part-time hovercraft engineer, had wallpapered his wife after an argument over a plate of glazed tuffles. She had bought a second-hand orang-utan and trained it to rape her husband. He started to like it and asked his wife for a divorce. Suddenly Mr Farrington vanished in an all-night launderette, and his wife was arrested on a charge of suspected murder and keeping a monkey on a low-fat diet.

I was called in by Mrs Farrington, whom I had known when she was working as a shepherd in Lambeth. We'd had a thing going between us in those days, until she'd met a ventriloquist in a holiday camp. One night I asked her to marry me, but she turned me down without moving her lips.

Needless to say, I had solved the Farrington Mystery, but it had been politic to give the credit for the solution to the New York Police Department.

I received a fat cheque for my trouble, and the orang-utan became a social worker.

Now, as then, I had to tell all, and I did. Mallet and I drank cup after cup of coffee as I told him the truth of what had occurred. We went over the events again and again.

We agreed that Mussels had not been involved in the murder of the old gypsy or the death of his mother, the bad nun, but we were no nearer to discovering who had killed 'Lucky' or Karl Jerome or poor Mrs Fettersfill – why had she been killed? Had Mussels seen her off? The evidence would seem to suggest that by the modus operandi ... frankly, I prefer an inside toilet. Another horrid thought crossed my mind. Would Mussels hold me responsible for his mother's death?

Mike Mallet fell asleep whilst I was crooning 'Moon River' and I tiptoed out of the office and prepared a light breakfast of suckling pig, aromatic herbs from Java, braised yams with raspberry leaves, iced spinach and mongoose livers on a bed of hot vindaloo sauce and oven-ready chips.

Mallet roused himself and threw up on the pig but managed to keep the iced spinach down.

As he was leaving the office, he stopped at the door – which was just as well because it was shut. He turned and said in a puzzled voice, 'Say, Marlowe, does the name "Happy Harry" mean anything to you?'

I thought long and hard, but couldn't think who 'Happy Harry' could possibly be. I shook my head. Mallet shrugged his considerable shoulders and said off-handedly, 'Some dame phoned the precinct and mentioned that name in connection with Jerome's murder, but we ain't come up with anything so far.' With that, he left.

I sat at my desk and idly threw peanuts at my cat. I've had that animal for years and I always thought it had one eye – now I suddenly realized that it was walking backwards. This case was getting me down, and it worried me because I don't suit duck feathers. Over and over the name 'Velma' came into my mind. It seemed to me that the whole case hinged on her.... But where was she? What was she doing?

I smoothed a piece of foolscap and picked up my pen, a goose quill. It writes beautifully but the problem is it's still attached to the goose. I wrote on the paper all the names concerned in the case, including those who had been murdered, and I still couldn't see any light at the end of the tunnel. I'll never have an office in a tunnel again.

I pushed the foolscap away in disgust and sifted through a pretty sordid assortment of mail. Bills and more bills ... I had more bills than a pelican farm.

I'd forgotten to pay the last instalment on my uncle's burial and there was a short letter from the undertakers saying that they'd dug him up, and he was folded up on a bogie in a goods yard. The last letter was from my ex-wife, Belinda. My stomach knotted. Belinda, even after ten years of separation, her name still stabbed my heart....

We had been so in love, Belinda and I.... Many women have passed through the portals of immortality: Cleopatra of Egypt ... Joan of Arc.... Add to those illustrious names: Belinda Gluckstein. That was her stage-name, her real name had been Freda Gluckstein. And what a dame – when I first met her, a tingle ran up my leg ... she'd scratched me with her bike clips.

When we met I was working as a Rabbi's assistant. It didn't last long – I wasn't really cut out for it. The wages were poor but I could always rely on tips.

In those days she was employed in Woolworth's. I remember I'd gone in the store to buy a doggie's pooh-pooh container; they were going cheap at the time and were not to be sniffed at. I had asked her about the possibility of a discount. I'd said, 'Hey, beautiful, what will you take off for cash?' She'd replied in a throaty voice, 'Everything bar my earrings.'

On our first date we sat holding hands on a bus, which took some doing – I was upstairs and she was down. I took her to a posh restaurant where the menu was written in French. I ordered 'Poulet de la Normandie aux Près.' The waiter shook his head and said, 'You can't have that, it's the band.' We laughed, and finished up with cod and mash.

It was there that I fell in love with her. I recall leaning across the table to kiss her lips by the light of the candle between us. She jerked her head away and I fell on the candle ... it took the head waiter fifteen minutes to get the wick from up my nose. That night in her flat she had whispered, 'Darling, I'm going to slip into something cool.' An hour later I found her asleep in the fridge.

We had a quiet wedding; there was a silencer on her father's rifle. Oh, the fun we had on our honeymoon.... The rock garden where we got stoned together, the way she pulled her purple knickers over her head and pretended she was a damson.

Our first little home was a bungalow, a split level bungalow. The living-room was intact but the kitchen was split. She was a lousy cook, bless her; one night she prepared for me 'Football Supporter Chicken.' I'm not saying what it tasted like, but I never watched Arsenal again.

One night she won a talent competition in a public house by dancing barefoot on hot dominoes whilst tearing a telephone directory in half. She was a hit, by golly, and I was so proud of my wife – until a theatrical agent signed her up to be a stunt woman on *Songs of Praise*. From that moment on, our marriage began to decline.... We slept on a water bed and we just sort of drifted apart. Her career was her whole life, and I was tossed to one side.

She appeared in the film *Gone With The Wind*. I didn't see her in that; by the time I got into the cinema she'd gone.

Ten years, and I still can't forget her. I read her letter. It was a short note asking me if I'd seen a tin of brown paint in the attic – apparently when she'd run off with an acrobat she'd forgotten to take it with her. That was Belinda.

I shakily poured myself a drink and opened a drawer in my desk where I kept all the photographs of our honeymoon. We'd had a white wedding; Belinda had come straight from night shift at the flour mill. I looked at the first photograph: she and I driving down the freeway. The next one was of a hitchhiker thumbing a lift. Then there was the photograph of the hitchhiker holding us up with a gun and driving away in our car. The next photograph was one of Belinda and myself hitching a lift.

There was a lovely photograph of her and a crocodile in a swamp – I took that one – and there was another of me and the crocodile – she took that – and finally one of Belinda and myself ... I don't know who took that photograph.

*

I sat there alone with my memories; where was she now, my lovely Belinda? I peered at the postmark on the envelope the letter had come in. 'West Borneo' it read faintly, and I thought, What the hell is she doing over there? Then I remembered: she had a sister who owned a club out there. I'd seen the club once, it was about three feet long with a nail through it.

Sadly I put the photographs back into the drawer and lit a cigarette, my fortieth that day. I've tried to stop smoking many times, I even went for acupuncture, but all the guy did was stick needles in my cigarettes. Instead of cigarettes I tried a bar of chocolate – useless, every time I lit the chocolate it melted.

Annie, my old char, stumped into the office with a bucket and mop. 'You're working too hard,' she admonished. 'Take a holiday, Mr Marlowe, you look ill.'

I nodded. 'Thanks, Annie. Believe me, when this case is over, I'll be off to the sun.'

Annie noticed that the drawer in my desk wasn't shut properly. 'Been lookin' at those pictures again, hey?' she said gently. 'You've got to forget her.'

Shaking her head, she walked away and started mopping up the mess the cat had done in the corner. As she did so, I heard her singing a strange, timeless sort of lament:

'There was a young girl from Hitchin
Who was scratching her bum in the kitchen.
Her mother said, "Rose, it's a rash I suppose",
She said, "Sod off, and get on with your knitting".'

There was something haunting about the song and I asked Annie where it came from. She leant on her mop, ran her fingers through her grey hair and thought for a moment, then she said, 'That was the signature song of H.H.Merrypepper, the music-hall act who fired lumps of cheese through his vest.'

I chided her. 'What sort of a stupid act was that?' I jeered.

Annie frowned. 'He was very good in his day, let me tell you.

'A funny man was Happy Harry....'

I sat stunned. *Happy Harry*, the name that Mallet had mentioned.

'What happened to him, Annie?' I asked, trying to conceal my growing interest.

She looked at me, scratched her head and replied, 'As far as I know he went potty after finding a starched rabbit in his road manager's surgical boot.' She finished cleaning up the cat's mess and went out of the office, still singing that strange song.

I phoned Mallet and informed him about Happy Harry. He thanked me and said he'd find out where the old performer was.

The hours ticked by, and I waited. This was the only lead we had and I wanted to follow it through. After what seemed an age – actually, it was only a fortnight and the clocks had gone back – Mallet rang me. 'Okay, Marlowe, write this address down.' As he spoke I repeated it, and we agreed to meet at the mental institution where Happy Harry was to be found.

Annie must have gone ages ago but, bless her, she'd left a slice of conger eel pie and a Gideon Bible for me on the stove.

Chapter Three

'I like golf because I can play a Round. I'm not bad at it, but I've a Fairway to go.

I never get hungry playing golf. I always have a Sand Wedge with me, and I can always stop for Tee.

Some beautiful women play golf; there's one in particular I've got my eye on, I'd love to Bunker.

Of course, I always play with something on my head, like a Handy Cap.

What Drives me on? Perhaps I'm a Chip off the old block – if you don't believe me, ask my Par.

I enjoy vegetables, I never tire of Greens, so Putt that in your pipe and smoke it.

For years I've worn the same socks but now there's a Hole in One, and that's the Bogie....'

Marlowe

Mallet was waiting for me outside the high wall that surrounded the mental institution. It looked a forbidding place, and I shivered.

He pulled on a rope that hung from the side of two massive iron gates. A bell clanged loudly. We waited in the swirling fog until eventually a heavily built man in a white uniform came crunching down the gravel drive. He had a face like a bull mastiff, then I realized I was looking at a bull mastiff on the end of a stout leather lead.

'What you want, hey?' the white-uniformed brute snarled. The dog lunged at Mallet and pee'd up my leg.

'Police business, Buster. Open up.' Mallet shoved his badge in the guy's face.

The man shook his mighty head. 'That's not a badge of police,' he growled.

Mallet looked at it and realized he'd shown him a Guinness label by mistake. It took him ten minutes to find his badge; it had dropped down his boxer shorts and he had to take his trousers off to retrieve it. Finally we convinced the man that we had an appointment and he admitted us through the gates.

The institution had once been a fine old house, but now it looked as if it was a time-share for a werewolf. The fog was so thick I tried whistling 'Moon River', but I couldn't find my lips.

Mallet and I were taken inside the building by a man wearing a fur hat and a grass skirt who said he was nearly cured. Later on we found out he thought he was a kipper. He asked us to wait in a small room that lay off the main hall, and he left us a pair of skipping ropes and a wind-up plastic frog to play with.

Mallet was uneasy, especially when another man, dressed in a suit of armour, asked him if he knew Gladstone. On the walls of the room were paintings done by the inmates; some were excellent. One in

Piece of halibut
tacked in
corner

"HOLE OVER SEPTIC TANK"
BY
EL CRAPPO
(1731–1951)

This priceless painting was to play a big part in solving the mystery. It was found floating on a bank of stew near a clown's hat.

particular caught my eye. It was a view of an old water buffalo's foot in a tube of custard – and I caught my eye on the tube which was sticking out from the canvas.

We heard the sound of high heels clicking towards us, and into view strode a tall lady, quite elegant in a wet suit and diver's helmet. She offered Mallet and me some minced meat from a bucket, but we declined and she seemed offended.

Again she offered us some minced meat from the bucket, and this time Mallet gestured that we should take some of the stuff in case we offended her once more and made her even dottier. Just as I held my hat out for her to sling some in, a tall nude man balancing a bowl of fruit on his nose shouted, 'Don't touch it – that minced meat is still alive!'

'Curse you, Waldo,' the woman in the diver's helmet screamed. She ran to a wall and stood on her head.

Mallet and I were frozen with fear, but the nude man gave us both a plum and indicated that we should follow him, which we did. To our relief, he took us into an office through a door marked 'Dr W. Theobald, Institute Director.'

We sat down, and the nude man went over to a cocktail cabinet and brought out a bottle of bourbon. Both Mallet and I said we'd love a drink, and the naked man rummaged for three glasses and poured out the fiery spirit.

'Let me introduce myself,' he said and wrapped himself up in a red flannel sarong before sitting down on a large comfortable-looking leather chair. 'I am Waldo Theobald, director of this mental institution, and you may find my ideas a trifle peculiar.' With that he jumped on top of the desk and started bringing canaries out from under his flannel sarong. It looked good, but the only thing was the canaries were on fire. He didn't seem concerned one iota, and went on to play a mouth organ as the canaries dashed round madly beating the flames out. He finally gave up and resumed his seat, but not before throwing a lemon meringue flan in my face.

'My theory is, gentlemen, that to seek the reason for insanity, one has to be one of the inmates, if you see what I mean. That way the cause can be more easily detected.' As he spoke he started pulling yards of ribbon from his mouth.

Mallet had had enough. 'Very unorthodox treatment, Dr Theobald. Have you cured anybody by attempting to be one of them?' He spoke sternly.

'No,' replied the doctor, 'but by jove I can dance the tango.'

We left him humming a passionate Spanish serenade and went to look for Happy Harry. Apart from a couple of Napoleons, a stout woman eating a newspaper, and a small chap doing something awful with a rubber thing, the place didn't seem busy. After a short survey, Mallet and I saw our man. We couldn't miss him: he had a big top hat on his head with an electric sign on it which kept flashing the name, 'Happy Harry'! In addition to the ridiculous hat, he wore comical boots, a red cloak and cardboard trousers.

When he saw Mallet and me, he bowed and boomed through a megaphone, 'Welcome to the show, folks. My name is Happy Harry and I'm the funniest man in the country, but not in the town. . . . Ha ha ha. What's brown and sits on a piano stool? I'll tell you – Beethoven's last movement. . . . Ha ha ha.

'My wife thinks she's a hen; I'd take her for treatment but we need the eggs. . . . Ha ha ha.

'Take my wife.... *Please.* She's so fat, when she walks on a zebra crossing, they have to jack up the stripes.... Ha ha ha.

'Talk about ugly, when she goes to a zoo, she buys two tickets – one to get in and one to get out.... Ha ha ha.'

A prickle touched a nerve in my mind. I shouted at him, 'Harry, didn't you love Velma?'

He stopped the jokes at once, shook his head and started crying. 'Do you know where my Velma is?' he pleaded in a hollow voice.

'Sure, Harry, but tell us about it.' I coaxed him gently.

Out poured the agony of a lost soul....

Harry was working the clubs in Oldham and going well with the hard-bitten Northern audiences. His Disappearing Kangaroo Illusion was a smash hit – nobody could work out where he shoved the kangaroo after putting it in a parcel of tomatoes.

One night his assistant, Marie, dropped dead when the horse she was carrying gave birth to twins. Harry had to find a replacement, and the new assistant came in the shape of the sultry Velma. She told Harry that she'd given up her job at the Manchester knacker's yard and had an Equity card.

Harry fell for her hook line and sinker, which she sold to a Latvian tree surgeon who caught a salmon with the tackle. Her beauty was the main attraction of the act, and to save money Velma sacked the seal and did the ball-on-the-nose trick herself. Everywhere they appeared, they attracted large audiences, and before long, it was obvious that Velma and not Harry was the star.

Poor Harry was besotted with her. She played him along with promises of love and a trip to the Lake District, and Harry believed her because he'd never been to the Lake District. It had to end in tragedy. One night, after their appearance at the Cocoa Rooms and Thermal Baths, Crewe, where Velma won a set of wooden teeth for charity, she flaunted her naked body to a window cleaner who didn't go out a lot, and Harry found them under the cleaning leather doing a crossword puzzle.

It was the last straw for Harry. The poor fool lost his reason and tried to blow up the Lake District. He was taken away by a nice man who gave him a string bag full of biscuits.

This was Happy Harry's sickening tale. A great talent destroyed for the love of a vamp, and a career that ended in a mental institution. Mallet and I were moved by his story, and as we both sat on the lavatory, I vowed that I would find and bring the accursed Velma to justice. The daughter of Satan himself, she had wrecked so many lives.

We left Happy Harry dancing and telling his little jokes to the midget who was doing something awful with his rubber thing. The good Doctor Waldo Theobald tried to sell us his feet as we sped away from that most depressing of places.

*

The following evening, I switched on the television set just in time to catch a news flash, and my gut knotted.... Happy Harry had been found murdered in the grounds of the asylum. At that moment, Mallet rang and told me that Harry's body had been found in the grounds of the asylum with a flute rammed up his anal passage.... I could only imagine the pain he'd suffered, and mentally thanked God that the murderer hadn't used a clarinet.

It was quite obvious that somebody knew every move I was making, and I simply had to talk to somebody.

I gunned my saloon down the motorway. Rain was sweeping across the city skyline, creating a glittering wet curtain in the neon glare. As the windscreen wipers rubbed backwards and forwards, I lit a cigarette and thought about Mussels Malloy, Velma, Karl Jerome, 'Lucky', and poor Happy Harry. I even thought about my mother's bread pudding. My mind was in a turmoil and I drove on and on, unconscious of the direction I was taking. It was strange how my thoughts turned into memories ... Things were coming back to me that I hadn't thought about for years. My lonely early childhood – the only friend I'd had was a water melon – yeah, sounds crazy now, doesn't it, but to a ten-year-old boy who had no friends, that water melon was a pal. I'd tell it little stories and it would roll all over the floor, I couldn't take it out for walks on a lead because it had no neck, and once when I put it under my vest and went on a picnic with it, my mother thought I'd got a pigeon chest and had me operated on.

A kid who lived on our block deliberately stood on my melon one day. I watched the life-water ooze from it.

The kid ran away, and I went to try and find a melon doctor, but there wasn't one in the Yellow Pages. When I returned, I knew there was no hope. My father was picking his teeth, and there were pips on his chin. That incident made me hate my father; how could he have eaten my best friend? I tried to find another soul mate at the greengrocer's. For a month I went out with a lemon, but it was vicious and went for the eyes. . . .

I suddenly realized that I was approaching the outskirts of Miresea-on-the-Crouch, and I knew that I needed to see Lola Vallance.

Miresea hadn't changed: the same old zebra crossing, its stripes looking a bit faded as it trotted across the road. The hotel I had stayed at was being picketed by smallpox victims, and a child had just shot his parents so he could go on an orphans' picnic.

I knocked on Lola's door. When she opened it, I stood shyly on the doorstep and said, 'Can I stay the night here?' She nodded and said, 'Of course you can,' and then she shut the door.

It wasn't very comfortable on the doorstep, but in the morning the milkman gave me a carton of cream and a doughnut. At ten o'clock Lola let me in. She sure looked cute in her short nightdress, and almost without thinking, I embraced her.

'Cut it out,' she rasped, so I cut the nightdress off and kissed her. We made love, and I blurted out everything about the case. She listened with an intent expression – it was the first time I'd made love to anybody in a tent

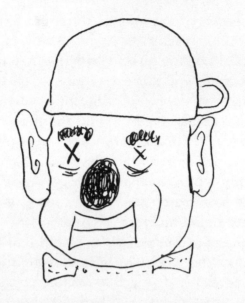

Death Mask of Happy Harry with a galvanized chamber pot on his head. Note the comical wax ears from a mail order company in Norwich. Widely regarded as an authority on prune juice, he could be easily moved. Born in a glove compartment, Happy Harry amused many people by eating his socks at Hitler's Christening.

with that expression. She looked beautiful as she lay nude on the divan mending a puncture, and it did me good to unburden myself.

When I got to the part of my story that concerned Happy Harry, she gave a little cry and threw the tyre she was mending at me. 'Oh my God!' she gasped. 'Death follows you everywhere, Marlowe.'

I left her sobbing and went into the kitchen to get her a glass of water. She must have been getting lunch ready because there was an ox rotating on a spit. She gulped the water and lay in my arms. 'Marlowe, it was I who phoned the police about Happy Harry...'

'You phoned the police?' I asked. 'But why, Lola?'

She beckoned me into the kitchen, and as she poured a sauce over the ox on the spit, I peeled the oranges before sticking them in the mouth of the boar's head on the sideboard next to the stuffed swan and glazed pheasant.

'It's a long story, Marlowe,' she said, as she sliced slivers of undercut from the cow hanging on a hook.

I didn't urge her to tell me her story. I boiled some lobsters for her in the cauldron and waited for her to compose herself, which she did, and a pleasant tune she composed as well. I watched her expertly dress a silver bowl with sheep's eyes and trout fingers in walnut chippings, and I knew I was falling for her when I slipped on a heap of bedevilled kidneys and fell on her.

We made love over the ox, were possessed by one another.... Finally our passion was spent and I hadn't got a credit card on me. Our love-making had made us hungry, so we had an ox sandwich, which was enjoyable except for the ox's leg sticking out from between the slices of bread.

Lola stopped chewing the rib-cage and told me about herself and Happy Harry.

'My brother booked Happy Harry into the casino,' she said slowly as she cracked her lobsters open with a sledge-hammer. 'Gee, he was good in those days, Marlowe. Every night I watched him make the kangaroo disappear, then saw the ears off a customer, and I'd marvel at his cucumber juggling. When the casino had closed, I'd stay talking to him for hours. I guess I got carried away with the glamour of show business because I let him make love to me one night on a roulette wheel. I begged him to stay in Oldham and I still think he would have done so, if that bitch hadn't come into his life.'

Lola stopped abruptly, she'd got a lobster claw stuck up her nostril. I tried to tug it down but it wouldn't budge. It didn't seem to bother her, and she carried on patting ox dripping into squares.

'Velma, that woman,' Lola hissed angrily, the lobster claw waving from side to side. 'From the moment he set eyes on her, Happy Harry forgot all about me, and that was that. It took me a long time to get over Harry.'

She was silent, and absently set fire to the lobster claw instead of her cigarette. I prised the claw out with pliers and took her in my arms, saying in a low, vibrant voice, 'I don't care what you did in the past, Lola, or who you loved. I only know that I am enraptured with your effervescent personification of feminine pulchritude. The very essence of corybantic amatory emotion is a maelstrom in my breast.'

'Bollocks,' Lola said.

We made love once more, then Lola finished off her story. It seemed that she had received a telephone call from a woman who suspected that Happy Harry's life was in danger. The name of the woman who had rung Lola was Mrs Fettersfill. This case was getting screwier by the minute: just how the hell did she fit into all this?

Lola explained. 'Mrs Fettersfill worked as an undercover agent for Weightwatchers, and it was there that she met Harry who was doing tricks for fat people who'd lost more than three pounds in a week. He persuaded her to go as his road manager and chef on his forthcoming tour of Lundy Island. She liked Harry, and as she was making herself ill on salads, she readily agreed.

'After his triumph in Lundy, they journeyed to Halifax where they both spent a terrible week one night.

'In Leeds Harry broke all records at a disco – he fell off the juke box, and Mrs Fettersfill was knocked down by a steam roller and had to stay in hospital in Wards Two, Three and Four. Harry reluctantly had to break off their relationship, and Mrs Fettersfill knew why.... Harry had a new girl assistant – Velma!'

Lola made some coffee, and when she'd stopped jumping up and down on the beans, she went on: 'Mrs Fettersfill knew the girl was no good for Harry – or any other man for that matter – but what could the poor woman do about it? She was lying in bed with doctors trying to pump her back into shape with air hoses, and she was helpless. She never saw Happy Harry again, although he did send her a Christmas card one Easter as a joke.'

I kissed Lola goodbye and left Miresea-on-the-Crouch before the volcano erupted.

I knew that I loved Lola as I had never loved Belinda, and I knew that I would return to Miresea ... I had to, I'd left my underpants and truss underneath the corpse of the ox.

The city was dark when I braked to a halt outside my

office. I went to unlock the office door – I've always found that's the best way to get in. I need not have bothered ... the door was open.

I retracted my steps and lugged my cannon out of the boot. I was taking no chances. With the help of three pulley wheels and a mule, I got the cannon into the office, primed it with powder and rammed a ball down the barrel.

I switched the light on. There was nobody in the little reception room, only my little receptionist, and she was dead – mind you, she had been for some time, but she was never one to complain.

Gingerly I made my way to the main office, switched the light on. Nothing, but there again I smelt that perfume.... I looked under the desk, over the desk.... Nothing had been disturbed, so why had the office been broken into?

Too late I realized I should have looked down at the side of the desk, because it was from that direction that somebody slugged me, and as before, I dropped into a black pit.

A blinding light in my eyes guided my return to consciousness. I tried to move. I couldn't. I was tied very tightly to a chair in an unfamiliar room. A voice at the back of me, a voice I remembered, broke the silence. 'So, Mr Marlowe, we meet again.'

I grinned mirthlessly. 'Well, well, Mr Vance, and how have you been keeping?'

I heard the man take a deep breath. 'How did you

know it was me?' the voice said. Emery came into focus, immaculate in coonskin hat, Inverness cape and see-through clogs.

'I'd recognize that voice of yours anywhere, Emery,' I snarled.

He looked long and hard at me. 'I don't want to hurt you, Marlowe,' he said, 'but my safety is being threatened by someone, and I think you know who that someone is.'

I attempted to struggle, but two big guys swam into view and leaned on me. 'Listen, Vance,' I said earnestly, 'I wish I could tell you what you want to know, but I don't know anything, and that is the truth.'

Vance chewed his bottom lip. 'I wish I could believe you, Marlowe, but I cannot take any chances. You'd better spill the beans or my two employees will beat it out of you.' He'd chewed through his bottom lip and had started on his top one. I knew the guy was scared. The tension in the room grew, and now Vance was asking one of the big guys if he could chew one of his lips. I decided to tell him what I knew, if only to play for time.

At the mere mention of the name Mussels Malloy, Vance paled and backed away into a corner. I seized on his fear and took the offensive by singing 'Moon River'. The two large men hummed along with me, and Vance begged us to stop by offering me a time-share in a villa in Lyme Regis. He was in a blue funk, which didn't suit him one bit . . . bright puce was his colour.

The two toughs implored me to sing 'Ticket to Ride', and I agreed on condition they untied me. They did, and we sang close harmony as Vance cowered in the corner.

We had a break from singing and I took the opportunity to ask why Vance and his thugs had broken into my office. He seemed surprised and said that the office door was open when they'd got there.

I left him and his gorillas with the promise of getting the two lads an audition, and a packet of Band-aids for Emery's lips.

Emery had left the keys in the ignition, so I got in his car and drove away. As I rounded a traffic island, a powerful paw gripped my shoulder, and in the mirror I saw the hulking outline of Mussels Malloy. Again my bowels turned to water.

'Keep drivin', Marlowe,' he boomed.

'What the hell are you doing in the back of this car? I gasped.

He leant forward, his breath smelt of burnt cabbage and cheap cigars. 'I was waitin' for Vance. I think he knows where my Velma is.'

My hands trembled on the steering wheel.

'Every cop in the city is after me,' Mussels said grimly. 'I gotta find my Velma – cute as lace pants, she is.'

I realized that Mussels was like a cornered animal, dangerous and wild. He lit up a stalk of burnt cabbage. 'Sorry about the stink, Marlowe,' he grated. 'I've run out of cheap cigars.'

Suddenly there was a wail from a police siren coming up behind me, and I realized that I'd forgotten to put my headlights on.

'You better lose the copper, Marlowe,' Mussels boomed in my ear and I threw out a handful of ten-pence pieces, but it didn't stop the police car drawing closer.

'Give it more gas,' yelled Mussels, and I belched even louder but I couldn't shake the cop off my tail. How I didn't have an accident I'll never know – I dodged and weaved through the peak-time traffic, and there were a lot of pekes about. Horns were screaming at me in rage as I darted back and forth to shake off the cop behind.

'Give me the wheel,' snarled Mussels, so I unscrewed it and handed it over to him in the back seat. That didn't help matters because Mussels only had a provisional licence. I braked hard and the car slewed sideways to a stop down an alley off the main street.

I replaced the steering wheel and reversed out into the main drag. There was no sign of the police car.

Mussels clambered out of the vehicle, and as he did so the cop car, lights blazing, came alongside. The copper got out and grabbed Mussels by his braces, but Mussels leapt back in the car and we screeched off, the copper in hot pursuit. I jammed my foot down and we catapulted away, but the cop car drew close, then came alongside – went in front – then suddenly flew to the back of us again. I couldn't believe it: this kept happening over and over again. I couldn't figure it out, then it dawned on me. The copper still had hold of Mussels's braces, so every time I got in front the braces stretched to their limit, then twanged back and hurled the cop car in front.

'Unfasten your braces, Mussels,' I yelled.

The big ape actually blushed. 'Can't you wait until

we've stopped?' he whispered tenderly. Luckily for me, there was a fretsaw on the passenger seat, so I lunged backwards with a sawing motion and cut the big lug's braces in half. It worked. The police car flew back, described a parabola and landed upside down on a bus full of Japanese tourists, and they took three thousand photographs of it. One of them bowed to me and said it made a change from the Red Indian.

On and on I drove into the night. 'Where the hell are we going, Mussels?' No answer. I asked him again. Still no answer. I braked and looked into the back seat. Mussels had vanished ... only his trousers complete with severed braces lay on the rear seat. My first instinct was to bugger off and get away as far as possible, and yet, oddly, I felt a certain responsibility for the big brute.

Sighing heavily, I reversed the car and drove back the way I'd come. It was not a nice area. There were brothels on every street corner and scantily clad women were giving me the big eye, but brothels ain't for me, I don't even like broth. Drunks were staggering all over the place, waving empty bottles, a queue of people waited to be mugged in a bus shelter, and a thin woman was jumping up and down with a sign on her chest which read: 'In case of sexual assault, this way up.'

My lips curled sardonically. So this is what civilization had come to. The thin woman had mis-spelt 'assault' as 'arsalt'.

As I observed the human decay, I thought of those far-off days on my uncle's farm. Uncle Hamish bred hamsters, which amazed everybody because normally hamsters do it for themselves. Dear old Uncle Hamish, his wisdom forged in the clean country air. I remembered the way we'd bounce together on a trampoline, each holding a bucket of milk until it turned to butter. He had a great respect for money, did Uncle Hamish, nothing was ever wasted. He once found a crutch so he went home and broke my auntie's leg. Many people thought he'd gone too far when he took the pendulum out of a grandfather clock in case its shadow wore a hole in the wallpaper. If a fly landed in his glass of whisky, he would hold the fly upside down by its neck, shake it and shout, 'Spit it out!'

Auntie loved him despite his apparent meanness, and even as she lay dying, she was thoughtful. The family gathered around the bed decided that the hearse and one car would be sufficient for the funeral. Uncle Hamish said there was no need for a car for the mourners, they could stand on the roof of the hearse to go to the cemetery. Then, having counted the cost, he decided that there was no need for a hearse either; the family could rent a plank of wood, fit two sets of roller skates to it and pull Auntie along to the graveyard. As they were assessing the cost of this new scheme, Auntie got out of bed and told them she'd walk to the cemetery.

With Auntie gone, Uncle Hamish became a philosopher. I remembered his wise sayings as I sat on his knee whilst he rummaged through my pockets for pennies. Here are just a few of those thought-provoking, sage comments:

'A wet owl on a dead carrot never flies in the morning.'

'A wasp on dung that's stuck to a riding crop in a tub of mole spit means a hot winter isn't always.'

'To wipe your granny's blouse on a rabbit's genitals is to deny the life of a turnip worm that is part of Nature's scheme to have youngsters in hot straw.'

At the time he told me these things I honestly thought Uncle Hamish was cracked, but as the years have rolled on I know now that if our poor demented world could live by his creed, it would be a happier place.... I'll never forget his last words before he passed on to that Great Wallet in the sky.... 'AAAGGGHHH!' – that's what he said.

I keep promising myself that one day I'll revisit the farm and allow the nostalgic memories to envelop my senses. Not many of my rustic relatives are left. Cousin Joab, the family drunk, died in a barrel of lager. Nobody really knows how much of the stuff he swallowed, but three weeks after he was buried you could still smell his breath at the inquest. The only plants that will grow on his grave are hops.

Cousin Rosie, dear Rosie, she became a sumo wrestler in Orpington but didn't vote Liberal. My little niece Gertrude (we called her Rude for short), married a cannibal and tried to convert him to vegetarianism. After an argument over a nut cutlet, he left his job at the swimming baths in Luton and all that was found of Rosie was one of her back fillings, her string vest and a strong smell of chutney. Years later the cannibal came back to the baths at Luton, and everyone was amazed how long he could stay under water at the deep end, holding his breath.

I watched him down there and said to an attendant, 'Isn't it marvellous how he can hold his breath for so long?'

The attendant replied scornfully, 'He's a bloody show-off, he's been down there a month.'

How strange the quirk of fate. He'd eaten Rosie in a fit of temper and tossed lettuce, and had come back to the scene of the crime to have his life as forfeit.

All these things were passing through my mind as I drove through that bad part of town. Corruption in every garish neon sign ... humanity sinking into an abyss of sin.... Then I saw Mussels standing in front of the Japanese touring coach, holding his shirt up as the dirty little Nips took photographs of his penis, and every camera was fitted with a zoom lens. I'm not saying he had a whopper but he looked like a tripod.

I swung myself out of the car, wrapped his thingy up in the car rug and dragged – or tried to drag – him into the car. 'Mussels,' I shouted, 'you'll have the cops here.' He seemed bemused, and all the Japs could say was, 'OOOOOOHHHHOOOOOOOO.' I was good and mad. 'Let go,' I screamed. 'It's not a yard of salami!' One hard-looking Japanese lady in a floral kimono went into a Kung Fu stance and said, '扎入 乩夭 井 文ぐ 尕ィ'

That did it. I remembered Pearl Harbor, I even remembered Pearl Bailey, and I wasn't being spoken to like that. 'Sod your transistors,' I yelled, and threw raw fish at her, followed by a wine list.

She dodged and hit me, and I went down like a sack of

flour. I staggered to my feet. 'What did you hit me with?' I gasped.

She said, ' 冗 朰 九 以 肀 灾 ' Which roughly translated means: 'Kung fu ju-jitsu high side foot kick to nerve centre of temple causing obstruction of blood to thorax.'

As she turned away to take another photograph of the Mussels Manhood, I smacked her across the back of her neck and she fell like a stone. When she came to she rubbed her neck, bowed and said, ' 宀 灻 朰 以 矢 ' Which means: 'What the hell did you hit me with, a karate blow?'

I snarled, 'No, Madame Butterfly, it was a 1939 Vauxhall coupé starting handle.'

Mussels was getting excited by all the attention and if he got any stiffer I knew I'd never get him back in the car.

I dropped him off at a seedy, run-down hotel with orders to stay there until I contacted him. For once the giant obeyed me and shuffled off into the grimy darkness of the building, which rejoiced in the name 'The Majestic Hotel'. I made a mental note of the address and drove slowly back to my office. Although I tried to dismiss it, an idea kept popping into my head, drilling through logic. . . .

Somebody knew every move I was making, and that somebody had to be close to me, but who?

Over and over I mulled the problem, and over and over a name came up: Annie.

I pulled the car up at the side of the road and lit a cigarette. What did I really know about my cleaning lady? Oh, she'd come to me with good credentials, but anyone could have worn them.

I thought back over the events. When Mallet had telephoned me about Happy Harry, maybe Annie was still in the office after all; nobody else could possibly have known which mental institution he was in.... I went back further in my recollections. That message from Mrs Fettersfill: Annie must have taken it at the office and passed it on to my hotel in Miresea....

Other little things came back to me: it had been Annie, I recalled with sudden shock, who'd carried the dead horse down from the office to the street, not the vet, because he said he'd got a bad back.

I knew nothing about her, I didn't know where she lived or what she did in her spare time.... Everything pointed to Annie being heavily involved. She knew all there was to know about my investigation into the Velma case.... Another strange thought struck me. *Could Annie be Velma?*

My heart was thumping a maddened tattoo, my mouth was dry, I had to find out more about my cleaning lady. I restarted the car – it goes much better when I do – and drove to my apartment, straight into a large gin.

Chapter Four

'There was something Fishy about the dame and I knew she had an Angle. . . . But she had me Hooked.

One night she told me to Clam up. If she ever does that again, I'll Bait her brains in.

Oh, she was Shellfish all right, and I was just a Prawn in the game.

She had no Sole; I knew that there would never be a Plaice for us, and it gave me heart Hake.

What was I to do? Am I my brother's Kipper?

There seemed to be no Porpoise in seeing her, but I've never been one to Carp.

Outside her house was a stile and I used to Perch there for hours singing 'Salmon of these Dace'.

She wore a Herring aid, and I wore a Cod piece.

She's going out with a guy but Eel never amount to much, he's from Whales, and one day they'll both Flounder.

What a life. . . . Nobody knows the Turbots I've seen.'

Marlowe

I awoke from a deep slumber. I must have slept like a baby because my big toe was in my mouth.

I heard a loud banging on my front door. I knew it was the rent-man because blood was coming off his knuckles through the letter box. Next he attempted an entry with a battering ram, but I ignored it and did my morning exercises — up-one-two-three-down-one-two-three, then the other eyelid.

I got in the shower and suddenly noticed how thin I was getting — I was having to run round under it to get wet. Since this case had started I'd virtually lived on alcohol and cigarettes. Small wonder, then, that the stones were dropping off me.

My wife, Belinda, had once lost three stones by swimming in a deep pool. I never understood why. I'd tied them around her neck tightly enough.

I had no coffee in, but at least there was a half-bottle of vodka in the fridge. It was still there. So was the body of my cat.

I dropped the bottle of vodka to the floor and it smashed into smithereens. My cat dead, and not only dead but stuffed with olives and Marmite! I couldn't believe it — I can't stand Marmite, it makes me trump.

Who the hell had done this? Was it a warning? I used to take that cat to the office and back with me most days; it had been my friend, and much nicer than the melon I once had. I felt an anger I'd never experienced before. Some bastard would pay for this: cats are expensive to start with.

Whoever had done this grisly deed had not escaped without a scratch or two — I saw some strands of wool from clothing adhering to the poor creature's claws, with a tinge of blood there as well, so the cat had scratched deep.

It was obvious that I was getting close to solving the case; somebody was worried, that was for sure.

I took the dead pussy to a piece of wasteland, but before I could bury it, a man bought it off me to use as a doorstop and draught excluder. He gave me a pound in ten-pence pieces and the address of his mother, who wasn't feeling very well.

Annie was in the office doing some bricklaying when I arrived. 'Hi, Annie,' I said in a forced cheerful voice. She took the hod off her shoulder, brushed her grey hair back, and for the first time I noticed the boa constrictor tattooed down her biceps. . . .

'Hello, Mr Marlowe,' Annie said. 'As soon as I've finished laying this thousandth brick, I'll make you a cup of coffee.'

I bowed theatrically. 'Thanks, Annie. What would I do without you?'

She grinned and wagged her finger at me, and placed the hod back on her shoulder.

I decided to set a trap. I dialled a non-existent number and pretended to speak to someone on the other end of the line. 'Yeah, I think I know who's behind all the killings. . . . Mussels Malloy? Naw, they haven't got him yet, but I've got a hunch. . . . Oh, you've seen my hunch? Doesn't bother me now, it did do, but I wear a crepe vest these days. Okay, I think something will give us a clue at the old Emery Vance place – 87 Park View Mansions – see you.' I put the receiver down, swivelled my head and saw Annie with an ear trumpet peeping round the door jamb. My hunch was correct: Annie was involved.

I left the office, banging the door noisily behind me, then took my shoes off and crept back. Annie was whispering to someone on the telephone. I couldn't hear any of the conversation, but now I knew who had been responsible for anticipating my every move.

When Annie left the office, I followed her on foot – it was my own fault, I'd forgotten the car.

She walked briskly and I had a job keeping up with her, but she seemed totally unaware that she was being followed. She stopped only once, at a tobacco kiosk, and it stunned me to see her buy a pound of Russian chewing tobacco and a copy of *Woman's Own*.

She finally stopped outside a block of apartments in a very swish neighbourhood indeed. The towering block was most impressive. How the hell did Annie manage to afford a joint like this on the dough I paid her? (I'd never given her money, she preferred dough.) I watched her go inside ... then I thought, Maybe she has another cleaning job? That seemed a logical explanation.

I didn't even know Annie's surname, so there was no point in trying to find which apartment she was in, and I didn't want to raise any suspicions by making inquiries about her. I was content for now to leave matters as they were. I returned to the office, stopping first at a wine shop to pick up some hooch.

Back in the office I downed a fiery tumbler of the vodka I'd just bought, and switched my answering

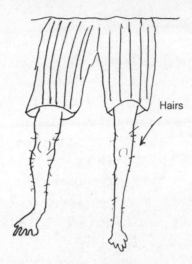

Hairs

Karl Jerome's own legs in striped candy family-sized boxer shorts from British Home Stores price £3.50. His legs proved to be the same age as his knees and brought Velma to justice. Sketch provided by passing upholsterer on a Morris roof-rack.

machine on. To my astonishment there was a short message from police headquarters saying that Mallet would be in touch with me soon. That didn't add up – what the hell did he want? I hadn't been in touch with him. I had another vodka but this time I didn't set fire to the tumbler.

Another message came on, from a lady who wanted me to find her husband. He'd run off with her mother to a dog track, taking her post office savings book, and bogus Krugerrands.

The last message was from Lola Vallance saying that she'd taken my underpants to a launderette to be cleaned and they'd refused them.

I gave her a quick ring, she's a kidder all right. There was no answer, and I felt a little disappointed at not being able to speak to her ... that dame had really got under my skin. I glanced at my watch – it's a habit I've got into when I want to know the time – the hour had arrived for me to spring the trap with Annie. If my hunch was right (although it sometimes leaned to the left), she would be at 87 Park View Mansions.

I decided not to take my cannon, instead I chose my telescopic lightweight alloy pikestaff, folding copper shield and packet of shark repellent. I wanted to be on the safe side. I shivered slightly; I wasn't feeling myself and it's never the same when you do. It wouldn't be long before this case was solved; I had that well-known tightening of the gut which from past experience meant that the gas cylinders had overheated in my truss and the toggle switch on the camphor valve mounting cam-shaft housing was de-threading the chrome screw on the propeller up inside my waistcoat pouch where the motor was.

87 Park View Mansions lay in darkness, and there was something evil about the place. Someone else had thought so, too, because the walls were covered in garlic and Bela Lugosi's name was in the rent book.

A faint breeze caused the branches of a dying elm to flutter, and odd rustlings in the thick hedgerow indicated that creatures were present.

I had difficulty getting out of the car because my telescopic pikestaff had shot out to its full length and wouldn't snap back into place. By dint of worming my legs over the pikestaff, my backbone was arched and my foot was trapped in the steering wheel. I inched over on my left flank but the gear stick went into my groin and burst through the zip on my flies.

I pulled myself backwards over the driver's seat, which collapsed, and I found myself upside down with my trousers now wrapped around the gear stick. Leaving my shoes where they were, I bent my legs until they were at right angles to my body. Using my free right hand, I contrived to wind down the window and fumble for the door handle. The door swung open and a rampant labrador jumped in the car and started making love to my leg. The dog's owner was a Japanese tourist; he took a roll of video film before getting the fire brigade to release me.

I pinned the car rug around my waist like a kilt and threatened the labrador that I'd have his licence endorsed. The Japanese owner of the infernal animal said, '㐆㐈'.

I knew what that meant: it was one of the most scathing insults only used in certain parts of rural Japan, and I kicked him in the hara-kiri. He knew he'd gone too far – he should have got off the coach at Wembley. He ran off with his dog into the night.

I crunched down the drive, fear tingling in every pore. The huge oaken doors were not locked. They creaked ajar ... I entered. The house was as silent and musty as a forgotten tomb. The musty smell grew stronger; a man in a black tail-suit approached me and the musty smell became overpowering.

'Who are you?' I asked.

'I'm Musty, the butler, sir,' he replied.

'What do you do here?' I said.

'I buttle, sir.' He bowed slightly as he spoke.

'Have you been buttling long?' I asked him.

'No, sir, I've always been the same size,' he said.

'I don't like you attitude, Musty,' I retorted.

'It's not my hat he chewed, it's yours, sir,' Musty said loftily.

I took my fedora off my head and saw that a badger had chewed the top off.

'May I take your coat, sir?' Musty said.

I shook my head and patted the badger's back to bring the wind up. 'No, Musty, I haven't paid for it yet.'

I didn't care for the man, he looked suspicious to me, and there was something about him that stirred my memory – nothing I could put my finger on, and there again I wouldn't want to, but something. . . . I dismissed him, but he'd had a good innings, and off he went home.

The house was still and I confess I felt on edge, so I got off the edge and walked into the great reception hall. My footsteps echoed on the marble floor, vast portraits glared down on me: long-dead celebrities, perhaps?

There was no sign of Annie and it looked as if I'd been wrong in my assumption. For no reason at all, except to keep the story going perhaps – and at present you couldn't keep it going with a pacemaker – I leant against a corner of the stone fireplace. I must have pressed on a switch or lever, because the fireplace swung open.

There was a room inside, full of cobwebs but no sign

of any cobs.... There was, however, the body of an elderly man in a vest, boxer shorts and spats, and my years of hard-boiled detection told me that I was looking at the remains of the real butler. Musty would never buttle again.

He had been murdered in a very grotesque fashion. Someone had put a funnel in his mouth, and judging by the number of empty bottles around the corpse, he'd died as a result of an overdose of brandy. There were two sets of footprints: one obviously belonged to the killer, and the other to Mr Musty. His footprints led to a toilet, so it was strangely apparent that he had been to the gents' at least once whilst he was being murdered.

What a fool I had been! I could have caught the murderer red-handed, instead I had sent him home.... Or had sent *her* home? Could it have been Annie dressed as the butler? I clenched my fists in an agony of futility, and it was agony – my cigarette was still lit.

Cautiously, I crept through the reception hall and into the dining-room. On the long, highly polished table were signs that somebody had had a recent meal. A half-consumed veal and ham pie jostled with a dish of plover's eggs and a platter of Écrevisses à la bordelaise 'Bois Joli', which was too overcooked for my taste.

The plate of Tournedos 'En Bite' in the centre was delicious but could have done with a pinch more rosemary.

The Choucroute Garnie au Champagne was a different kettle of turbot altogether, and the Knockwurst and Saucisses de Toulouse defy description.

The Poulet à la Marengo, the pastry bouchées and

what was left of the Jambon Chaud à la Chablisienne 'Alexandre Dumaine', I awarded eight out of ten, but not for the Pears In Pastry or the Sabayon. Incidentally, the mushy peas were crap.

From the dining-room I entered the library, which was a tone poem in Georgian elegance marred by the body of a housemaid lying under a sun bed and still soaking wet. To my trained eye it was instantly obvious that she had been poached to death.

In all my years as a private eye, I had never encountered such a bizarre set of murders, and I knew I was up against a cold intellect who would stop at nothing. As I stooped over the body of the poached maid, there was a lingering smell of perfume....

I ran up the stairs and sprawled my length over yet another corpse ... the body of a traffic warden. What he was doing there I'll never know, but he had a parking ticket stuck up his arse.

Of Annie there was no sign, and in a way I felt glad that my hunch was incorrect, because a good cleaning woman is damned hard to find these days, as well you know.

I picked the telephone up and dialled the police. Mallet was out on a case so I asked the desk sergeant to put me through to Ted Conway, whom I'd known since we played together as kids. I liked Conway, he was a straight shooter and he sometimes gave me free tango lessons at the baths. Ted was a great athlete, the captain of an underwater polo team, and he was a good, plodding type of cop.

The mansion was getting on my nerves and the reek of

death was in the air. So was a low groaning sound coming from the library. Carefully I sidled into the ornate room. There was nobody in evidence. Again I heard the groan. It seemed to be coming from behind an oak-panelled wall of leather-bound books.

I pulled some books out, pressed the panels, knuckled the walls to see if I could find the entrance to a secret passage. I was just about to give up when the police arrived. Ted Conway shook my hand; when I took him on a tour of the murders, he paled and his eyes went like saucers, which wasn't easy because Ted's Chinese on his mother's side.

I told him about the groans coming from inside the library, and together we tried to find the secret entrance. It was Ted Conway, accidentally placing his hand on a copy of *Lady Chatterley's Lover*, who discovered the key. Ted hadn't read the book before so I pointed out the tasty bits, which made him excited and keen to get back to his wife.

As he put the book back there was an audible click, and a section of the panelling moved to one side, revealing the semi-conscious figure of my cleaning lady, Annie. She had been bludgeoned by something heavy and her hair was matted with blood.

I cradled her head in my arms while a cop brought a bowl of water and a cloth. There was a gleam of recognition in her eyes when I spoke to her, and she beckoned me closer. Unable to speak, she traced some letters in the dust of the floor; they seemed to form words: 'Tell me', was it? Or possibly 'Tell ma'?

'Tell me what, Annie?' I whispered.

She flopped out again and a stern voice behind me said, 'Okay, Marlowe, suppose you fill me in on what the hell's going on here.'

I looked up at the authoritative figure of a very angry Inspector Mike Mallet.

Four of us carried Annie out of the secret recess. We laid her flat on the settee. 'The ambulance is on its way,' I heard a policeman say softly, but he knew and I knew, as indeed we all knew, that it was too late for Annie. It wasn't just the blow on the head that had done it; a Cornish pasty had been thrust down her throat and she was already flaking to death.

Again she beckoned me closer. Her voice was faint and I couldn't make sense of what she was saying. Suddenly her eyes opened wide for a split second. She looked around and gave a gasp, and then Annie, my cleaning lady, one pound fifty an hour with own bucket and leather, was gone.

The tears flowed and I held her tightly. There was so much I wanted to say to her – how well she'd taken care of aspidistras in the office loo, how well she'd done the bricklaying and small bore engineering.... I'd never be able to replace her. I smoothed her grey hair back and saw that she had a pig's ear in place of one of her own. I was stunned, to say the least. Just then, a rather elderly policeman bent over and when he saw the pig's ear sewn on her head, he said in a trembling voice, 'That's no lady ... that's Gaylord Malloy!'

I took the grey wig off to reveal the close-cropped head of a man. The nose, I suddenly noticed, was made of clay. I pulled it off, and the real one turned out to be as flat as a pancake.

The elderly copper told us a very strange story.

Gaylord Malloy, Mussels's father, after running away from home had earned a living wrestling with a bear in a circus. Part of his gimmick was to play a violin before entering the cage; the music soothed the animal and made it easy for Gaylord to wrestle with it. One day the circus owner found the bear dead after trying to mount a giraffe, and so as not to lose Gaylord, he replaced the bear with another one.

That night, before a packed house, Gaylord played the violin. The bear stood stock still, Gaylord entered the cage, and the bear bit his ear off. It turned out that the new animal was tone deaf.

The surgeons couldn't sew Gaylord's ear back so, with his permission, they put a pig's ear in its place. Three months after being released from hospital, somebody said to Gaylord, 'How is your hearing these days?' Gaylord replied, 'Not too bad, my own ear is fine but the pig's ear – well, I get a lot of crackling in that one.'

Such is human nature, people laughed and scoffed at his pig's ear, so he grew his hair long and went in a sideshow as 'The Human Ape'. One day, to his horror, he saw his son Mussels looking at him in revulsion (or it might have been Newcastle), and he watched his son drop to his knees and sob with mortification (who was his best friend).

All this now explained why Mussels had cried when I called him an ape. That incident sent the boy demented, and his father, reading about the crimes in the paper, knew his son was responsible.... He had created a monster.

Gaylord had been an atheist for years until he realized he was getting no holidays. Now his conscience pricked him and he set forth to find the meaning of life. From the lips of a Nepalese lorry driver, he heard of a monastery in Tibet: the monastery of Kali-pu.

He withdrew his savings from the Abbey National and set sail for the East. The voyage was abysmal – scurvy, a mutinous crew, beri-beri – but at last they reached Knutsford.

He arrived in China, had his head shaved, donned saffron robes, and was chatted up in a pub by a well-dimpled tea planter. At last, after climbing the Himalayas clad only in Bermuda shorts and a saucy singlet, he found the monastery, and even better, the head monk, a two-hundred-year-old lapsed Baptist from Lewisham. The old wise man was sitting on a large stone gazing into the far distance.

Gaylord fell to his knees before the ancient sage and said, 'Oh, Wise and Noble One, who is attuned to all things natural and without deceit, thou who hast lived many springs, tell me the Meaning of Life. Tell me, what have you got from sitting on this boulder?'

The old man raised his eyes to heaven and said, 'Wisdom, compassion and piles.'

Gaylord returned home a wiser man, and determined

to look after his son's interests and to try to steer him away from a life of crime.

After learning that Mussels had been to see me in an effort to find the dastardly Velma, Gaylord disguised himself as an old woman and became Annie, my cleaner. In that way, he reasoned, he would be in a position to help his offspring and one day be reconciled with the mighty moron.

Gaylord was not an educated man; one of the reasons for his ignorance was that he suffered from dyslexia, but in other ways he was kayo.

When the elderly policeman had finished his story, I'd aged considerably and he was now eligible for his pension.

Gaylord's body was taken away and I found myself more bemused than ever. Long after the police and medics had departed, I still remained in that house of death mulling over all that had transpired. I was far from solving the case and yet ... in some way I knew that I wasn't. The solution had to be right under my nose, along with the nostril hair and the pimple.

Driving back to the city was a nightmare, I'm not into horses, but seeing a mare driving at night was kinda weird.

My office welcomed me with its usual musty odour of gin, tobacco and debt. I threw myself into a chair and looked out of the window at the neon-lit metropolis; a cesspit of human corruption.... Pimps, hookers, crooks, deviants, killers, dope pushers, insurance salesmen: my city, my streets.

The phone jangled into life. It was Mallet. 'Marlowe? Thought you'd want to know, that client of yours, Mussels Malloy, we've got him cornered in a joint on 5th and 10th.' With that slice of illuminating repartee, the telephone went dead.

I sighed. Here we go again, I said to myself.

I left my car outside the office and grabbed a cab to 5th and 10th, which lies just off 4th and 6th; they run across 7th and 8th Street past 3rd and 2nd. Turn left at 3rd Street and you're in 12th and Randolph, but I don't know where he runs.

The flop-house where Mussels was holed up should have been condemned by the Pilgrim Fathers.

If ever the authorities decided to demolish it, they would have to repair it first so that it would be safe to pull down. The windows were so filthy they needed cleaning with a Brillo pad. It was the sort of dump where you set the mousetraps with smallpox vaccine. The last time it was painted, Rembrandt did it.

The police were crouching behind their cars with pistols, machine-guns, tear-gas, hand-grenades, family-sized truncheons and bars of soap. The slum was lit by searchlights, and Ted Conway was holding a megaphone in his hand.

'Hi Ted,' I whispered. I looked around. 'Where's Mallet?' I asked him.

'Mike's out of town on a case,' he replied.

Suddenly the big head of Mussels Malloy appeared in the glare of the searchlights and everybody ducked as he fired off several shots.

Conway shouted through the megaphone, 'Give yourself up, Malloy, we've got you surrounded.'

Mussels reappeared and shouted back in a strangled voice, 'I want to see my daddy.' With that, he fired off a torpedo.

I turned to Conway and yelled, 'Where the hell did he get that from?' Conway shrugged and said Malloy had mugged a submarine earlier on. I knew that only starvation would winkle Mussels out. If the police attempted to charge, they'd be cut down in a hail of bullets, or the cockroaches would get them.

'Ted, let me go and try to reason with him. After all, he's my client and I feel responsible for him in a way.' I spoke with feeling. Conway simpered and said that I shouldn't be feeling him.

The police opened fire and the night exploded. The reek of cordite made you retch.

I backed away from the circle of cars and made my way to the side of the building. The alleyway was deserted. I had no difficulty in jumping up to bring the fire escape ladder down ... as I did so, a bullet whistled past my ear, and a figure darted into the shadows.

I climbed the ladder and broke into one of the rooms that lay beneath the one that Mussels was trapped in.

The room stank. It was so dirty, the carpet had a pulse.

A woman in a red surgical belt and bandoliers crossed over her chest was tickling a little naked man with a set of feathers. He was tied to a bass drum; there was a castanet taped round the end of his whatsit. On his head he wore an Austro-Hungarian Hussar's helmet with a sixty-watt bulb flashing on and off every time she tickled him. I thought at the time it was all very peculiar. I've never tried it that way, with a sixty-watt bulb on the helmet.

I mumbled an apology and gave them each a 'Singalonga Max Bygraves' song sheet.

The gun-fire was deafening as I crept up the flight of stairs to the room where Mussels was at bay.

I had no idea of what I was going to do; all I knew was that I was going to try to save the life of an innocent man. . . . Yes, I now knew beyond a shadow of a doubt that Mussels Malloy had never killed anybody.

I needed just one more piece of evidence, and I could then unmask the real murderer.

Mussels had his back to me as he sat crouched over his howitzer shells. Softly, so as not to frighten him, I hummed 'Moon River' in Dutch. He turned and saw me, and tears ran down his face.

'What am I gonna do, Marlowe?' he said, the tears flowing even faster as he peeled the onions for the piece of liver lying in a frying pan.

I shook my head angrily. 'Always peel the onions under the tap, you fool. That way it doesn't affect your eyes.' God, I was mad at him, the liver was burnt and there wasn't enough fat 1n the pan.

As Mussels buttered some slices of Pennine White, I put my head through the window and shouted for Ted

Conway to come up to the room and bring a couple of free-range eggs with him.

Half an hour later after we had finished the liver and onions – not forgetting the eggs – Mussels put the kettle on and we enjoyed a pot of Earl Grey.

During a respite, I filled Conway in on what I had discovered, and he went pale. 'If you're right, Marlowe,' he gasped, 'it will blow the lid off this city.'

Conway was great; he agreed with my plan to get as many of the suspects as possible up to the Vance villa in the hills, and there I promised to identify the killer. Conway urged me to go to the district attorney with the solution; I disagreed, I wanted him to come to the villa.

I sat in my office, set my plans, then quietly drank and smoked a large part of the night away. I was satisfied that my hunch was right, and to make sure it stayed there, I bandaged it tight to my right shoulder.

What had once been a hopeless case now seemed so simple; the answer to it had been there all the time, a story of greed and passion that had resulted in so many deaths and an article in *Reader's Digest*.

Conway had taken Mussels to a safe address. I didn't know the address, but Mussels was inside a safe.

Such a little thing had given the killer away, so little I hadn't seen it until Annie's body had been found, and the words of an elderly policeman clinched it all. Even I found the whole thing almost impossible to believe, and I had to go over all the evidence again and again to convince myself that I was right.

I doused my head in cold water as the time for the final showdown grew near. I was nervous, I admit; what I was about to do would shake City Hall to its very foundations.

I left the office – no pointing taking it with me – that's just a little joke, and I doubt if it will ever be anything else but that. Still, as my Uncle Hamish used to say as he sat in a loudspeaker, 'Laughter in a distillery is like chalk rainbows, all white.' What a depth of meaning there is in that saying.

I drove slowly towards the Vance villa. The night was clear and the moon shone down with his merry smile. It was a night for lovers, not for the task I had, and I wasn't offended this time when the same bull terrier exposed himself again.

The moon glowed a halo over the sprawling villa, and I saw that Conway had done his part. The driveway was full of cars. The suspects were there.... The time had come.

I switched the engine off and glided down the driveway. I wanted to peer through the French windows and scrutinize my suspects and their behaviour.

There was a wide chink in the curtains and he was selling pre-packed duckling with orange sauce, but I opted for the spare ribs and chicken with lemon.

As I munched my quite enjoyable meal, I covertly watched the suspects in the huge ornate lounge, and I could sense their discomfiture. Ted Conway had done his part well. Mussels was handcuffed and chained to the wall with six beefy coppers around him.

Waldo Theobald was sitting in a chair, chain smoking. Such was the state of his nerves – why else would he smoke a chain?

Lola Vallance was draped on the chaise longue, her long, silk-clad legs sending out invitations ... she sure was a looker.

Emery Vance was pacing to and fro, his hands clasped behind his back. Dr Schmekel was drinking a glass of what appeared to be vodka, and the two cops from Miresea, Lauren and Hardie, had guilt written all over their faces.

'Piggy' Valdez was lying on the carpet trying to look up Lola's dress; that was tasteless enough, but he was using a telescope. Finally there was Freddy, the DJ from the local radio station in Miresea. He looked more than a little apprehensive....

So there they all were, and as I accepted a finger bowl from the wide Chink before he closed up for the night, I felt a deep sense of satisfaction. If my reasoning was correct, this case would be the making of me: I'd be a big shot and have enough money to buy things that I'd always wanted, like a back door and a bed ... and Lola would be mine.

I checked that I was wearing my bullet-proof sleeves (I hadn't been able to afford the full jacket). I ground my cigarette out on the gravel path, sucked in a long deep breath, opened the French windows and walked into the room.

For a brief moment there was a stunned silence at my

Java based designer top with wet starched banana strips on glazed dung pom poms

The pearls

Somebody's foot

Royal shrunken head

Stewed grass kilt

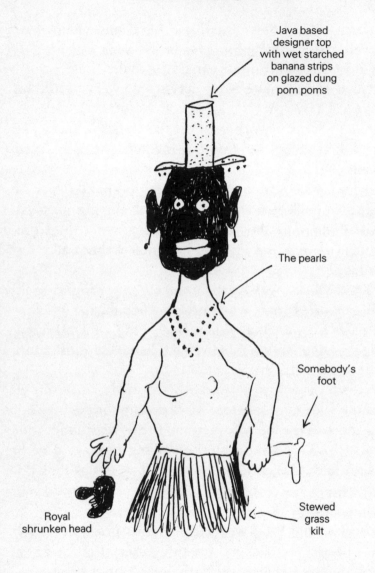

King Pittipoopi in traditional dung and banana hat. He is wearing the infamous pearls at a Jewish welders' rally in a Bing Crosby lookalike parade.

entrance, then they all started shouting at once. I gestured them to be quiet. I went across and shook Ted Conway's hand. 'Thanks, pal,' I rasped.

He looked at me. 'Jeeze, Marlowe, I hope you're right.'

So did I.

I made them all sit down – I wanted to heighten the drama and to accomplish that, I needed to take the floor, as it were. I lit another cigarette and leaned nonchalantly against the ornate desk that stood in front of a wall of books. I began my story.

'Once upon a time, there was a great king and his name was Ram the Elder. As kings go, he wasn't so hot, but he did have one thing ... a set of priceless pearls.' I paused for effect and blew a ring of smoke into the air. 'It's quite a story how he got them,' I went on slowly, and as I unfolded the tale the centuries rolled away.

Three times the young slave had been made to plunge into the lagoon by his masters; twice he had found nothing, and his lungs ached and his head swam. A whip across his shoulders forced him into the depths of the lagoon for the third attempt.

The youthful diver knifed downwards to the bed of the lagoon; this time he entered an underwater cavern, and saw what he had been instructed to find – a giant oyster. At last the discovery of the Pittipoopi pearls was at hand.

Pittipoopi, a South Sea Island chief, had hidden the pearls inside the shell of the giant oyster during a raid by a neighbouring tribe. Although tortured with hot irons, boiling oil and spear thrusts, he managed to die quite quickly, but not before putting the curse of dismemberment on the raiders. One hundred warriors lost a leg each that day, and a missionary hell-bent on rape lost something far more important.

After bringing the oyster to the surface, the young diver saw everybody hopping about and raced into the undergrowth, where he put it into a safe deposit box.

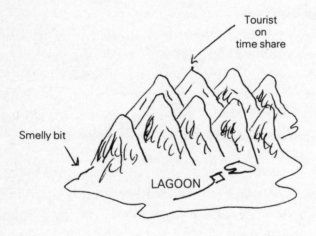

Primitive island where the pearls were discovered. In 1495 the island was turned into a shirt factory for a Spanish supermarket in Durham. The wages were low and the natives tall which led to rampant inflation and the use of stilts. A god-fearing foot specialist opened the first tin of salmon here and crossed a prostitute with an elephant – he produced a two-ton raver who did it for peanuts.

The oyster lay there undetected for over fifty years, until a relative of the diver who'd first discovered it took the safe deposit box home, fully intending to use it as a sort of ancient microwave oven. When he got the box open he threw the oyster away, but his wife wore it as a hat for Hallowe'en. The curse struck; during a spirited polka she high-kicked, and her left leg flew over the dancers' heads and hit the drummer in the band.

A Roman gladiator with two pumas and a Christian to his credit, went on sick leave and bought the oyster at a bring and buy sale in aid of Nero's violin bow resin. He had it for about a month before his elbow dropped off. He sold it to a merchant, who had an idea something wasn't quite right when the wheels of his caravan fell off.

Somehow the oyster turned up in Cairo, and it was given to one of Ram the Elder's concubines. From all accounts she was a nice enough lass but a bit on the big side; every time she bent her knees her eyelids flew open. Ram intended to get rid of her, but the girl's mother had shares in a pyramid and made the most wonderful dormouse flambé.

The concubine bent over one day and her bottom fell off; the curse had struck again, but the girl was delighted. Her figure looked better than ever and she became a papyrus centre-fold. Ram took her to bed and she was so grateful for a bit of the old nonsense, she presented him with the oyster.

One night Ram threw it at her and the pearls spilled out, but before he could whoop with joy, both his ears came away and his nose fell off the first time he blew it.

For the remainder of his life Ram wore a billy goat's head and insisted that his kids be brought up by a nanny, which everyone thought was a hoot. When he passed on, the pearls were entombed with him and the curse was extended to cover anyone breaking into the tomb, as well as touching the pearls.

His concubine opened a gift shop and ice cream parlour and lived to a ripe old age until they buried her – and they had to, she'd been dead quite a while.

'This, then, is the background to a tale of greed and deceit,' I said when I'd completed the story. My audience was enthralled. I've never seen an audience so

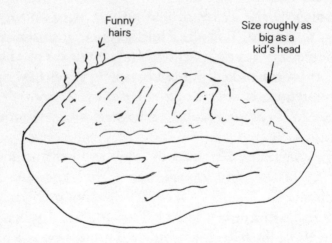

Funny hairs

Size roughly as big as a kid's head

Example of a Polynesian oyster from which came the pearls of death. The native name for this type of oyster is 'Maha Nā Goo Goo' which means 'Big Sod'. Found only in deep waters, the oyster finds mating very difficult and prefers to read about it.

enthralled; even the way they snored sounded enthralled. In fact, I was a bit enthralled myself, because only once before had I delivered a speech in public, and that was at the Bisley Rifle Club's annual hot pot supper. Afterwards the Bisley Riflemen presented me with six inscribed silver bullets – I still don't know what's written on them because I haven't yet dug them out of my chest.

I motioned for them to wake up by singing 'Moon River' from up on the chandelier, and I freely admit it, I climbed up the light fitting for one reason only – to peer down Lola's blouse. I swung back down on to the carpet. I had their full attention now.

'So we have the scenario, or the background, if you like, for this baffling case.... A string of pearls that carries a curse ... those who have handled it find themselves losing limbs and the like, so it was obvious to me that none of you, my prime suspects, had the pearls or had even handled them, because you've still got all your bits intact.'

That brought a gasp of admiration from the assembly. Ted Conway had a tear in his eye ... I was standing on his foot. Casually I mixed one of my favourite cocktails, one I call 'Ball in the Air' - if you drink more than one, you throw up.

'Little did I know when Mussels Malloy came to see me in order to find Velma that I would be involved in such a strange business. Like everybody else – including the police – I might add, I was fully convinced that Mussels was a cold-blooded killer. I know now that he never killed anybody.... Oh, he's mangled a few, but he's no murderer.'

My suspects gaped at me in wonder and Lola, bless her forty-five-inch beauties, stammered out, 'Then who is the killer?'

I lit another cigarette, forgetting that I already had four in my mouth. I sold one of them to Ted Conway and gave the others to be auctioned by a Pope look-a-like who was welding a ballcock in the cupboard.

'Who is the killer?' I paused. 'Good question, Lola, but first let me explain the chain of events.' I went on to explain how a chain had links and so forth, but I could see that I was losing their interest.... I continued.

'Mussels Malloy had two doting parents. His father, Gaylord, ashamed of deserting him, disguised himself as my cleaner, Annie, and kept his eye on his son. Gaylord figured out who the real killer was and paid for it with his life. Malloy's mother became chief suspect as far as I was concerned when she went around as the bald nun on horseback.'

Mussels gave out a long moan. 'Jeeze, Marlowe, was she my mummy?'

I nodded sympathetically. 'Yes, Mussels old son, you should be very proud of her. She came top in the convent pole-vault and the Mother Superior never once beat her at backgammon.' Mussels wept silently. I patted him on the head. 'Remember the mornings you woke up and there was a cup of tea and a Garibaldi biscuit on a plate? You always thought the horse had brought them into your room, didn't you?' Mussels nodded. I went on, 'It was your mummy all the time, it was she who looked after you, because, my dear

misunderstood friend, it was *Velma* who killed everybody and hoped that the blame would be placed on your
shoulders.'

The whole room quivered at my word. 'Yes,' I added.
'Velma is the murderer; a monster more evil than Satan
himself. When Lola's brother found the string of pearls
in the tomb of Ram the Elder, we all know, of course,
the terrible consequences. In due course the pearls
became an obsession with Velma. Cast your mind back,
Lola, to the casino in Oldham, the night the lame Dutch
goose-sexer threw a bucket of beetroots over an elderly
Wren who was dancing on the rim of a wet tuba.'

Lola leapt to her feet, her lovely face flushed. 'Why, of
course I remember that night, it was the night my
brother's arm fell off whilst he was playing snooker, and
someone tried to use it as a cue.'

I nodded. 'Correct, Lola, and the person who picked
up your brother's arm was Velma. She didn't want to
use it as a cue – she had a rotten handicap anyway – she
wanted to use it to steal the pearls with – that way, she
wouldn't have to touch them herself, and so she would
evade the curse. Can you remember where the pearls
were that night?' I asked Lola urgently.

She nodded her head vigorously. 'Yes, I can – they
were around my brother's neck. He'd put them there
during his Alice Faye impression.'

I finished my cocktail. Slowly I commenced to pace
around the room as I marshalled my thoughts.

'We can only imagine how many times Velma tried
for that string of pearls, and I strongly suspect she
seduced "Lucky" into the bargain, but no dice.... So,

our ever-lovin' Velma persuades Mr Karl Jerome to try to *buy* the pearls from "Lucky", who she knows is in financial trouble.

'Meanwhile "Lucky" discovers that Velma is stealing parts of Oldham to sell to a film company that makes horror movies on the side. She tells Mussels that "Lucky" has attacked her in the buttery and hopes the story will spread. Mussels is so in love with Velma he sets out to rearrange "Lucky's" body – what's left of it, that is – but Velma wants him dead, so she does the job herself, steals the pearls, then gets back into the disguise that has fooled us all.

'She moves to Miresea-on-the-Crouch as a dance director with a funeral company, and there she meets our two friends, Lauren and Hardie, the ever-willing cops. For a large sum of money and a leg over they agree to hire another bent copper, and meet Karl Jerome. What they don't realize is that Jerome doesn't have the pearls; what he doesn't know is that they don't have them either; get it?'

Everybody in the room shook their heads. 'No,' they said.

I carried on talking. 'After she killed "Lucky", Velma put the string of pearls into an envelope and sent them off to the main post office in Miresea, where Wells Fargo still has an office. It is obvious that she intended to doublecross both the cops and Jerome, but I think Jerome was on to her little game and that is why he hired me to act as a bodyguard.'

Lauren spoke up. 'But why use Hardie and myself and

the other cop to meet Jerome? Don't make sense to me.'

'She was determined to implicate as many people as possible. She knew that one day her connection with "Lucky" would come out and she couldn't afford that. You have to remember that Velma is quite insane, and has been ever since her uncle pushed her off a raft in the tunnel of love at Margate. For two years she thought she was a pilchard and tried to bomb Sardinia. Her parents sold her twice, but then she was taken into care after throwing Domestos over a clergyman. She was fined heavily for a Bleach of the Priest. Finally, after varnishing a bag of land army sandals and passing them off as Congolese suppositories, she was taken to a mental institution – the institution run by our friend here, Dr Waldo Theobald.'

The silly sod rose to his feet, in fact his feet were full of roses, and he started wallpapering a swan.

Ted Conway took the swan off him and I hid his teeth.

'Velma's biggest problem is Mussels; he has been constantly in search of her ever since his release from prison. She is forced to kill and kill again, but still Mussels evades capture. What is more, the pearls she has stolen turn out to be fake. 'There was no way that "Lucky" was ever going to wear the real ones again, after his arm fell off, and you, Emery Vance, knew that didn't you?'

Vance leapt to his feet at my words. 'Don't pin any rap on me, Marlowe,' he screamed.

I shoved him back in his seat and yelled, 'I wish I

could pin a rap on you, you rip, but you're no killer.'

Vance sat there, deflated, so there was no point in trying to pump him.

Ted Conway came over to me. 'Marlow, are any of these people here guilty of anything?' he asked quietly.

I nodded. 'Don't worry, Ted. Emery Vance is a blackmailer and a fence. Lauren and Hardie are both bent coppers – just look at the way they both lean; and Waldo Theobald hasn't paid his TV licence.'

Ted's face went ashen. 'The bastard,' he said through gritted teeth.

At that moment I felt sorry for Ted: there's nothing worse than grit in your teeth. I glanced at Freddy, the disc jockey. He had a smug expression on his face. 'Don't think playing a disc gets you off the hook, I know you've got a record.' That remark changed his expression.

Dr Schmekel shuddered under my piercing gaze. 'Oh, and by the way, Doctor, apart from the charge of abducting me –' I said, and he snarled, 'I never charged you for the abduction, it was on the National Health.'

I laughed a tight little laugh. 'What about those back street vasectomies you did in Warsaw?' He shivered. 'I have positive proof that you used blunt scissors on a package holiday tour operator who booked you into a hotel in Leeds and told you it was the outskirts of Barcelona.'

Schmekel lunged at me but I hit him with the dining-room table and Conway put the cuffs on his thin wrists.

Lola jumped up and cried, 'In the name of God,

Marlowe, where is Velma now?'

I didn't reply straight away. I gestured to Conway, who then took Mussels out of the room. 'Have you heard enough, Mike?' I shouted, and a very grim-faced Mike Mallet walked into the room.

'Yeah, thanks, Marlowe,' he replied. 'Lola Vallance, I arrest you for first-degree murder.'

Lola's face crumpled. 'What the hell are you talking about?' she screamed at him.

I looked at them both and drew a deep breath. 'Ted!' I shouted. 'Bring Mussels back in.' As I spoke I strode over to the light switch and turned the dimmer up fully. The room was almost bright enough to blind the eyes, and for the first time I could see all the faces clearly.

Mussels came in.

'Mussels,' I said gently, 'Velma's here.'

The giant blinked his eyes and looked around, and then I saw the most wondrous expression on his face as he saw her. . . .

'There she is, Mussels,' I said. 'Your Velma, or as she prefers to be known – Mike Mallet!'

Mussels tried to embrace Mallet, but he backed away, pulling his gun out. 'Get away from me, you stupid ox, I swear I'll kill you like I did all the others.'

Mussels still had his arms outstretched. 'Velma, cute as lace pants, why did you do me wrong, Velma?

Mallet fired his pistol; he'd been wanting to get rid of it for years. Mussels staggered and fell to his knees, but it gave Conway and me a chance to grab Mallet – or Velma – and take away the gun. Lola cradled Mussels's head; Waldo Theobald was reading a poem to the swan;

REAR VIEW OF
VELMA

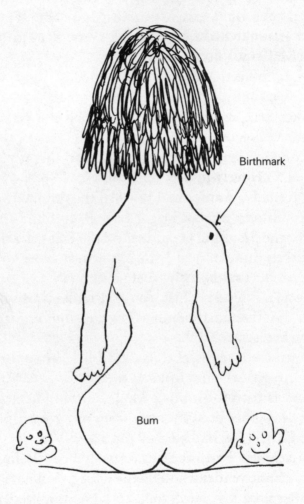

Birthmark

Bum

Rare sketch of Velma performing a scene from 'The Trial of Martin Luther' at a Dulwich garden centre. Her use of nudity in close-up magic got her a nice review in the *News of the World* and her blackheads cleared up.

and I smelt that elusive perfume as I grappled with the murderer.

The fight went out of Mallet, or as we knew now, Velma. I snatched the wig from her head, and long blonde hair fell down in ringlets. Suddenly defiant, she shrugged off her trousers and shirt, and there was the most beautiful woman I have ever seen. And to think I'd once washed her back.

'How did you figure it out, hot shot?' Velma grated.

I lit yet another cigarette. 'The credit, my dear Velma, goes to an elderly police officer who recognized that my cleaning lady, Annie, was in fact Gaylord Malloy, who suffered from dyslexia.'

Velma, beginning to struggle again, screamed, 'How the hell could that have given me away?'

I couldn't help but smirk as I replied, 'When we found Annie … I'm sorry, Mussels, I mean Gaylord, your father, he wrote in the dust, "Tell me" or "Tell ma".'

Conway scratched his head. 'So what, Marlowe?'

I put my face close to Ted's. 'Gaylord knew Velma from the old days, and when he saw her dressed up as Mallet, with his dying strength he blew her identity. Remember, he was dyslexic, so "Tell Ma" becomes "Mallet".…. That's how I knew who Velma really was, but it seemed so ridiculous I had to have Mussels to make a positive identification.'

Lola spoke up, her voice full of admiration. 'Great job, Marlowe, but how did you know about my brother losing his one good arm?'

'I didn't, Lola. I guessed,' I said softly. 'He had a withered arm, but that didn't fit into the pattern of the curse, and as he had handled the pearls, I assumed that something else apart from his leg must have dropped off at some time. I was in the toilets with him, and all his equipment down there appeared original, so I guessed it was the other arm that went.'

When I'd finished, Conway looked thoughtful; at least I thought he looked thoughtful. 'One thing puzzles me, Marlowe,' he said reflectively, then put the mirror down. 'Where are the pearls now?'

I shook my head. 'I've no idea, Ted, and I hope they never turn up again ... for they truly are the Pearls of Death.'

Velma spat at me as they took her and the others away. 'You bastard, Marlowe,' she screeched. 'I should have killed you first.'

'It's the chair for you, Velma,' I said. 'In fact, with all the murders you've committed, you should get three chairs.'

Mussels waved a piece of his vest and shouted, 'Three chairs for Velma.'

My heart sank when I saw the way Lola and Mussels were behaving on the settee; I'd lost her, I could tell by the way they looked at each other.

What the hell, I thought, I'm a private eye, a loner, there could be no room in my life for a dame. I'd proved a man innocent, I'd unmasked a killer, made love to a lovely woman.... Not for me the ordinary day-to-day existence, and yet what might have been if my marriage had worked? Even on our wedding day there'd been trouble; we had separate cakes for a start.

Lola and Mussels were at it, and I had to throw a bucket of water over them, but what the hell, I would probably have done the same. I left them writhing on the carpet, and I noticed three wild rabbits taking notes.

I let the tension ooze from my aching frame as I drove back to my office. The air felt good and clean, and another killer was safely under lock and key.

My office was dark and quiet and welcoming. I poured out a large vodka and gave myself a toast for a job well done.

Annie's mop and bucket lay in the corner, and my poor old cat had left a last mess. I switched the answerphone on; there was a call from the chief of police congratulating my solving of the case; a call from a man whose wife had gone out to buy a cabbage for dinner in 1963 and hadn't returned home, so I made a mental note to tell him to open a tin of peas; and lastly, to my astonishment, a call from Annie – sorry, I should say Gaylord.

The message was brief: an instruction to me to look under the toilet seat.

I couldn't understand why, but I dutifully went into the toilet, fully expecting to find a cleaning agent or something.... I flipped up the lid on the loo and saw a package Sellotaped underneath the seat.

Gingerly I opened it – I say gingerly because that cat could crap anywhere.... What I saw when I had unwrapped the package took my breath away. It was the string of pearls.

They were the most enchanting things I had ever set

eyes on; clear, sparkling, beautiful artefacts of Mother Nature, it was little wonder that so many people had lusted after them.

There was a note in the package:

'Dear Marlowe,

If anything should happen to me, these are yours. I found them by accident when I was steam ironing what I thought were my son's underpants, but then I realized that they would never have fitted round his bum. I didn't touch the pearls because they say there's a curse on them. Thanks for the Christmas bonus, Marlowe, and there's a spare bottle of Jeyes' Fluid in the cupboard.
Regards,
Annie.'

I broke down and wept because I thought I'd lost that bottle of Jeyes' Fluid, and because I would never see Annie again.

Carefully I emptied the string of pearls out on top of the desk. Oh, how they glowed . . . such lustre, I couldn't take my eyes off them. There before me lay riches beyond the dreams of avarice. . . . I thought of all the things that I could buy if I sold those pearls. . . . I would be able to go on all the rides at the Pleasure Beach at dear old Blackpool; I could have a villa in Cannes, any woman I fancied, and a hand-built truss with three-ply elastic and a non-wrinkle gusset.

No more detective work, no more worrying about unpaid bills – I'm rich, do you hear? Rich! Ha ha ha. . . . Wait, what about the curse? But no, this is the age of technology, Marlowe, men have trotted about the moon, we can transplant hearts and in some cases obtain interest-free credit. Even to think of anything as primitive as a curse is idiotic.... Wait a minute, what about what happened to the others who touched the pearls? Naw, it must have been coincidence.... Ha ha ha ... Marlowe, they're yours for the taking.... RICH RICH RICH....

My hands are trembling as I reach for them ... I'm now touching the string of pearls with my right hand ... ha ha ha.... Nothing's fallen off, no sirree.... Ha ha ha.... Rich at last.... The pearls are clenched in my right hand ... all mine ... the curse hasn't worked.... AW, SHIT!